My Magic Square

A NOVEL

Arianna Snow

Golden Horse Ltd.
Cedar Rapids, Iowa

This book is primarily a book of fiction. Names, characters, places and incidents are either products of the author's imagination or actual historic places and events which have been used fictitiously for historical reference as noted.

An *Original Publication of Golden Horse Ltd.*
P.O. Box 1002
Cedar Rapids, IA 52406-1002 U.S.A.
www.ariannaghnovels.com
ISBN 10: 0-9772308-1-3
ISBN 13: 978-0-9772308-1-5

Library of Congress Control Number: 2006925821

Printed and bound in the United States of America
by Publisher's Graphics, LLC

Cover: Design by Arianna Snow
        Photography by Rachael McClenahan
        Layout by CEZ
        Printed by White Oak Printing

Dedicated with love and gratitude to:

God

and the readers

of

Patience, My Dear

for the

inspiration to write this sequel

♥ my love and special thanks **to:**

CE

everything

KAE and RE

editorial

(Did you catch it the first time?)

DA

word processing

SV

computer aid

LC HR MH MP SJ

marketing

LS

love

Agnetta Inga-Maj Garpesjo-Davis

Swedish Language Assistant

♥

HIRAM GEOFFREY MCDONNALLY FAMILY TREE

PATERNAL GRANDPARENTS

CAPTAIN GEOFFREY EDWARD MCDONNALLY

CATHERINE NORTON MCDONNALLY

FATHER

CAPTAIN GEOFFREY LACHLAN MCDONNALLY

UNCLE

EDWARD CALEB MCDONNALLY

MATERNAL GRANDPARENTS

ALEXANDER THOMAS SELRACH

SARAH GLASGOW SELRACH

MOTHER

AMANDA SELRACH MCDONNALLY

SISTER

HANNAH RUTH MCDONNALLY

NAOMI BEATRICE (MACKENZIE) MCDONNALLY FAMILY TREE

PATERNAL GRANDPARENTS

JEREMIAH NORMAN MACKENZIE

OCTAVIA HILL MACKENZIE

FATHER

NATHAN ELIAS MACKENZIE

MATERNAL GRANDPARENTS

JAMES HENRY SMITHFIELD

IRENE CLEBOURNE SMITHFIELD

MOTHER

BEATRICE SMITHFIELD MACKENZIE

BROTHER

JEREMIAH JAMES MACKENZIE

STEPMOTHER

DAGMAR ARNOLDSON MACKENZIE

The Chapters

Chapter 1

"The Beginning"

"All my past life is mine no more;
The flying hours are gone,
Like transitory dreams given o'er
Whose images are kept in store
By memory alone."

—Lord Rochester

On October fourteenth 1913, Hiram Geoffrey McDonnally left the foothills of Scotland, surrounding his home, McDonnally Manor to begin his new life on an extended holiday in London. Although alone, he was determined to enjoy what God had to offer, whether it be a pea souper or sunny day. The tall, stately gentleman, with a head of silken black curls and ebony eyes, seldom walked the cobblestone streets unnoticed. His striking features and tailored wardrobe of the finest fabrics drew stares from those of all walks of life.

Adapting to life in London was slow-going for the modest man, having been a recluse for over eighteen years, but he soon learned to cope with the unwelcome eyes and hushed comments of those passing by. He became increasingly comfortable with simply offering a smile or a benign comment about the weather, rather than ignoring the curious admirers.

Hiram often strolled to the square to have breakfast at one of the quaint cafés, followed by a tour of the shops; today was such a day. After an early meal of hot tea and tarts, he spied an art exhibit centrally located in the town square. A number of local and visiting artists proudly displayed their oil and watercolor paintings. A notably attractive woman, of about his same age, was busy straightening the paintings which were propped against crates at her feet.

Hiram watched the diligent artist with interest as she moved gracefully about her designated area at the south end. She continued rearranging smaller canvasses on the two wooden tables standing on either side of a worn, green, ladder-back chair. Hiram approached her area cautiously, surprised to find that at closer range, her work was quite amateurish and lacking any notable redeeming qualities. At a safe distance, he examined each of her fourteen pieces with a mission to find but one example of satisfactory artwork. However, after a thorough examination, he discovered that the vendor's second-rate artistry was quite out of place at the exhibit, as the other dealers' creations were far superior in design, color and rendition. The disturbing reality of her failure as a painter urged Hiram on to the next artist. Hiram spent three quarters of an hour at the exhibit, before he left empty-handed and undeniably concerned for the woman who was, for obvious reasons, unsuccessful in her sales.

The town crier echoed at the end of the street announcing the funeral notice for a local resident, followed by the broadcast of the current feature *Queen Elizabeth,* starring Sarah Bernhardt, at the nearest cinema. To alleviate his preoccupation with the artist, Hiram attended the show, which ultimately failed as a diversion. He then walked to the nearby bookstore with a fine stone front and a sharp window display to visit with the proprietor, Daniel O'Leardon and then to join him for the afternoon meal. With the jingling of the tiny brass bell, dangling above the shop door, the owner's eyes left a stack of invoices and welcomed his favorite customer.

"Cheers, Hiram! I have some new editions ya might be likin'."

"From where were they shipped, this time, Daniel?"

"America. New York, lad," the storekeeper announced proudly.

"That's capital Daniel," Hiram solemnly responded.

"Yer ent'usiasm's overwhelming me. What's keeping ya up at night, Hiram?" Daniel questioned with his usual brotherly, sympathetic concern. Hiram took a deep breath and exhaled with a disconcerting expression and no commentary.

"I'll be fetchin' me hat and coat, Hiram." Daniel's tuft of red hair flashed past through the bookshelves and disappeared into the backroom. There, he informed Oliver, his young apprentice, to watch the shop while he stepped out for consultation and a bite to eat with his friend.

Meanwhile, Hiram flipped through a copy of Beatrix Potter's *Peter Rabbit,* then *Tea with Princess Penelope* that lay before him on a small oval table at the end of one of the aisles. The child's picture book was a collection of poems with elaborate corresponding sketches of animals, garbed in formal attire, preparing to visit a beautiful princess. On any given day, Daniel would sell at least one copy of this humorous book to an amused adult, supposedly for gift-giving purposes. Hiram, on the other hand, thumbed through the pages without cracking the slightest of smiles.

These animals look like animals. This illustrator probably never struggled a day in his life, Hiram thought. He snapped the book closed, agitated by the inequities in life, mentally revisiting the woman at the exhibit. Daniel reappeared beside Hiram patted his shoulder and led the way through the shop door.

"Smashin' book, ay, Hiram?"

Hiram shook his head, to his friend's dismay.

En route to the café, Hiram paused to catch another glimpse of the woman at the southern exhibit. Just as he suspected, she had not sold one of her paintings. She was sitting stoically, stiffly positioned in the ladder-back chair while an air of despondency hovered over her as her associates made record sales during the noon hour. Daniel, waiting patiently for his friend to reveal the source of his irritation, noticed Hiram's uncommon interest in the woman.

"Poor lassie, she's here ev'ry spring and fall and I've yet to see her make a sale. Happens all the time; no talent, no sales. 'Tis sad for all that witness it...starvin' artists, they be. C'mere, Hiram. I'm thinking ya be needin' a bit of tae, ye'r a wee peckish, that's all." Daniel motioned, noting that the depressing sight was adding little to his friend's morale, and a bit of refreshment would give him a lift.

Hiram nodded with knitted brows as Daniel ushered him into the restaurant. Hiram's appetite was lost, but he forced down the kidney pie, in an attempt to provide good company for his dear friend who ate heartily. During the meal, Daniel gave detailed summaries of two recent novels and then finally inquired to his companion's obvious distress. Hiram showed no inclination to discuss the troubling matter. After the relatively quiet meeting, Hiram accompanied his friend to the bookstore and bid him farewell.

Like Hiram, Daniel was a bachelor, but several years older. He lived comfortably in the flat above the bookstore. The Irishman had befriended the Scot from that first minute when Hiram returned to the London flat. It was located near Hiram's paternal Grandmother's home where he had spent most of his childhood. Daniel was by no means offended by Hiram's silence, having discovered over the past weeks that although his new friend was quite congenial, he was likewise a very private man.

Hiram returned to his flat. He placed his gloves on the bookcase in the narrow entry, removed his muffler, hat and coat and hung them on the tree stand. Lost in his thoughts of the distressed woman in the square, who sat cold and weary with disappointment, he prepared his fire. He poked at it a few times, then leaned back and watched the tendrils of fire begin to leap sporadically between the coals. Hiram soon dozed off dreaming of his visit to the square.

Nearly two hours had passed when he woke with a start. A hand gave his arm a tug. "Mr. McDonnally."

"Mrs. Yonnovich?" he queried as he squinted at the familiar face of his landlady from the flat below.

"You didn't answer after I knocked. I hope you don't mind, I used my key. I was a bit concerned and really needed to talk with you."

"I'm quite fine, Mrs. Yonnovich, the fresh air probably got the best of me."

"I wanted to remind you that we shan't be having supper in tonight. Mr. Yonnovich and I are leaving to visit my brother Jimmy in Edinburgh. However, I will bring your meal by at five, before we leave."

"You need not go to the trouble. I can go out for dinner."

"No, no, you stay in out of the cold by the fire."

"Very well, enjoy your evening with Jimmy, the fellow with the tall tales, as I remember. Fine chap."

"Yes, that would be Jimmy. Sorry to inconvenience you for a few days."

"Not at all, I meant to tell you earlier that I will be returning home to Scotland for the St. Andrew's celebration. So you see, your timing could not be better."

"How lovely for you; enjoy your journey, Mr. McDonnally."

"Thank you. Enjoy yours as well, and tell Mr. Yonnovich that we will continue with our dart tournament when I return."

"He will be glad to hear it. Good day, Mr. McDonnally."

"Good day, Mrs. Yonnovich."

Chapter 11

"The Engagement"

The path of love is both long and short.
For love is clear, pure, and bright, subtle,
yet simple, strong, diligent, brilliant,
and abounding both in
fresh thoughts and old memories.

—Raymond Lully

A cool November breeze swept across the moors of McDonnally Manor. Edward McDonnally, Hiram's kind-hearted uncle, repositioned himself with a nagging uneasiness in the large overstuffed, cabbage floral chair. He sat at his nephew Hiram's estate, curiously watching three animated women huddling on the adjacent window seat. The trio was discussing the prospects of the youngest, Allison O'Connor becoming the future Mrs. Guillaume Zigmann. The eldest of the conspirators, Eloise, the manor's housekeeper and proud mother of the "groom", delighted in the highly probable union. The dreamy-eyed blonde, Allison, sat engrossed in the conversation next to her adoptive mother, Naomi McDonnally.

Edward's focal point was Naomi, his wife in name only of eighteen years. After Naomi's tragic accident, for which he was partially responsible, Edward proposed marriage to rescue Naomi from certain life as a poor spinster. The unsightly scar which disfigured the side of her face was truly invisible to his adoring eyes. She had accepted the proposal, feeling her future was grim with her altered appearance and desertion by her first love, Edward's nephew, Hiram. Knowing Naomi's heart belonged to his nephew, Edward only provided the necessary financial stability for Naomi and daughter. However, a recent reunion proved that Hiram and Naomi were to share nothing greater than friendship. Since then, Naomi and Edward's bond tightened with each encounter.

Although their past meetings were infrequent, Edward had fallen silently in love with Naomi at the onset of their marriage. His dreams, choreographed by the Almighty, finally danced their way into reality when Naomi declared her love for him, only a few weeks earlier on Duncan Ridge. His greatest aspiration now, was to end their blossoming courtship with a second, yet perfect proposal. He believed that his beloved Naomi deserved the very best; that they needed a fresh beginning to renew their vows in celebration of their newly found love.

Edward eavesdropped on the women's prenuptial conference, in search of clues and general direction, being one with wedding plans of his own. He peeked over Wilde's *The Importance of Being Earnest* watching Naomi, who was apparently thrilled to have Guillaume, her former poetry reading companion, for a future son-in-law. Edward agreed, believing that Guillaume was a moral, responsible young gentleman.

After several minutes of bits and pieces of matrimonial information clouded the air, Edward fled to the kitchen for a glass of juice to quench his thirst and clear his head. He excused himself quite unnoticed.

"Mummy, he hasn't even proposed yet," Allison smiled shyly.

"My dear baby, Guillaume has been in love with you since he first heard your name. You have no idea how excited he was to meet you."

"He was counting the days 'til your arrival," Eloise chimed in.

"Mother, what type of man falls in love with a woman whom he has never met?" Allison questioned skeptically.

Eloise jumped to defend her son, "Why a fine gentleman indeed and not a more loyal beau to be found. Even when he was engaged to..." the defending mother's eyes widened and mouth snapped closed, caught in a trap of illicit information. All eyes turned to the older woman whose hand quickly covered her mouth to avoid divulging any further. She scanned the pathway to the arch, like a pursued mouse seeking escape.

"Eloise, I wasn't aware that Guillaume was engaged previously," Naomi questioned, as though she had misheard her friend's unexpected comment.

Allison leaned forward scowling slightly, focused on the informer's face.

The panicked housekeeper blurted, "I shouldn't have spoken a word about it. I promised. I am such an old fool." Eloise wrung her hands.

"Promised, Eloise? I'm sure Guillaume will understand and he may actually be relieved that Allison knows the truth." She turned to her daughter and smiled fearfully, aware of the progression of the young girl's thoughts.

"I doubt it," Allison retorted. "Guillaume had no intention of sharing the details of his secret life with me. I am obviously not privy to that information."

"Oh, no Miss Allison, it's not a secret. Guillaume was waiting for the opportunity to explain it to you, himself," Eloise pleaded.

"Well he didn't. We've been seeing each other every day for two weeks!" Perturbed, she left her place on the window seat and marched over to the divan. Eloise rushed to her side to affirm her son's innocence.

"Miss Allison, he spoke of it only last night at the supper table. That's why it was so fresh on my mind. The truth be told, he is a bit reluctant about discussing his past with you."

"That proves he has no faith in me; he's just like Hiram! They both think that I am not capable of coping with anything!" the young girl added defiantly.

"Allison. Please calm down," her mother cautioned with respect to her dear friend.

Allison snatched up a copy of *Vanity Fair* from the parlor table. She flipped rapidly through the periodical, while the older women considered the best possible means of diffusing her rage. Naomi approached her distraught daughter and hugged her reassuringly.

"Allison, this is not about Hiram. You know that Hiram is not to be blamed; granted the situation was misfortunate for all of us. But he will be here soon and you need to be civil to him. He has allowed us to remain here as guests and I am certain that you don't want to spoil the wonderful celebration that he has prepared. As for Guillaume, his past is just that, passed. Right, Eloise?" She turned to the older woman for support.

"Well, not exactly..." she muttered squeamishly. "I can't say anymore," she wrung her hands once again and then straightened her apron.

Naomi, shocked by the unexpected response, raised an eyebrow and pursed her lips, preparing to speak, but unable to find the words to console her daughter. Allison lifted her widening eyes from the magazine that slid through her fingers to the floor and stared aghast. Naomi observed her simmering state.

"Allison... I think that we need not speculate any longer on Guillaume's intentions." Naomi redirected the discussion, "What style of wedding dress do you desire? Only the best for my baby," she said forcing a smile.

"Yes, Miss Allison, what's the latest London fashion?" Eloise interjected lightly.

"I shan't need one! Excuse, me!"

In the kitchen, the dachshund littermates, Naomi's Heidi and Eloise's Rusty II, awoke from their basket and successfully begged at Edward's trouser cuffs for a treat. Edward then scooped up the two to return to the parlor when Allison flew out, cutting the corner to the stairs nearly taking off Edward's left arm. She charged briskly past him en route to the guest room on the second floor. Edward whirled around, clutching his canine passengers in surprise. He stumbled into the parlor to find further discordance with Mrs. Zigmann apologizing to his wife.

"Dear me, Mum, I never meant to upset her."

"I beg your pardon ladies; it appears that Allison is fit to be tied." He resumed his place in the large chair with the two puppies, which squirmed and circled to find a comfortable position on his lap.

"Not to worry, Edward, I will handle it. Eloise, it's the initial shock of the news. I will talk to her." Naomi lay a comforting pat on her friend's shoulder and sought after her agitated child.

"Anything I can do to help, Eloise?" Edward chivalrously offered.

"No, Sir... I got myself into this; I will have to dig my way out."

"Might, I throw you a shovel?" Edward grinned.

Eloise smiled gratefully, for the comment. Edward was one of those special people in the world, blessed with the ability for unzipping every black cloud to allow a ray of sunshine to pass through.

"Excuse me, sir. I have to find my son."

"Chin up, my lady." Eloise's countenance and posture resembled more that of one facing the "firing squad", which at this time was clearly commanded by her son.

"Don't fret. These things have a way of working themselves out," Edward called after her, "whatever they are... well, pups I guess we are better off distancing ourselves from this one. Back to my dilemma, why is it so difficult for a man to ask his wife to marry him?" he chuckled. He ran his large fingers gently over the long floppy ears of his companions. "I think that I need a new plan." Heidi whimpered disagreeably. "True, I never had an old plan."

Edward slid down into the chair and struggled to lift his feet with the wriggling weight onto the ottoman before him. Heidi and Rusty snuggled under his arms in the now peaceful parlor. Edward considered several locations for his future 'proposal'; all of which were lacking in one respect or another.

"There is something unnatural and complicated about proposing to a woman, who has shared your name for nearly two decades," he explained to Rusty. "And it doesn't help having a future father-in-law who wants to see your head on a plate!" he turned to Heidi's concerned face.

Oh dear God, help me with this one. His eyes fell shut pleading. *How can I make a second pro-*

posal special? It has to be one of the most wonderful days of her life.

It had taken all the courage that he could muster up to ask her to breakfast a few weeks ago, for fear that she would reject his invitation. Their first kiss on Duncan Ridge was nearly more than he could bear, knowing that Naomi McDonnally was at long last truly his. Edward sank back as he remembered that glorious day.

"Oh, Naomi," he spoke softly.

"Yes, Edward?"

Edward straightened with a sharp jerk, waking the two pets from their nap, nearly flipping them to the floor.

"Naomi! Uh...how is Allison faring?" He covered his startled reflex.

"Edward," she dropped down on the ottoman beside his feet, "it seems that every time one thinks that all is well, a new situation arises."

"Isn't that the truth?" Edward concurred, considering his matrimonial matters.

"Eloise disclosed inadvertently that Guillaume was engaged previously and Allison is convinced that his silence on the subject was deliberate."

"More than likely it was, Naomi. Sensitive subjects need to be addressed with careful consideration to time and place. Guillaume had obviously not found the proper of either as yet." Edward commented with seeming authority.

"Eloise assured Allison that Guillaume had every intention of discussing the details. I suppose that one would expect Allison to be taken aback, having received the information secondhand from his mother," Naomi determined.

"Unfortunate for the poor young man, deprived of the opportunity to choose the perfect time and place."

"Well, how could there be a perfect time and place in this situation?" Naomi asked inquisitively.

"What are you insinuating? Of course there can be a perfect time and place." Edward withdrew defensively, scooting the dogs from his lap and stood leaving them to share the available space on the chair.

"Why Edward, I only meant that it would be a difficult situation for both Allison and Guillaume, no matter where or when," Naomi offered diplomatically.

"Yes, yes, Naomi. Allison and Guillaume will be fine. They will get past all this. They belong together, I'm certain of that."

"Do you really think so? They are very young and impulsive and I am leery of Guillaume's ability to handle Allison's independent temperament."

"Better that he's familiar with the challenge now, than after they're wed. A man needs to know what he's up against before he lays down his life for a woman."

The dual reference in his statement shot an implosion of guilt throughout her body; *you sacrificed most of your life for Allison and me.* Naomi dropped her head in shock, considering that after all these years; he may be regretting his good intentions. A confused look befell Edward's face as she moved slowly, burdened by the weight of the implication. Once in the shadow of his looming height, she peered up, distraught with concern.

"Edward... I gave you so little in return for all that you have been providing for us. I realize that I have never repaid you... but ..." Edward's brow furrowed with each word and he slowly shook his head. *What is she doing now? I wasn't referring to my life!*

"I...I thought you understood the depth of our gratitude, we..." Naomi burst into tears and ran sobbing from the room.

Edward took a helpless breath and began to call out to her when he spotted Heidi making a daring attempt to leap from the chair to the ottoman. Edward immediately determined that the distance was too great and rushed to its aid. He snatched the dachsie in mid-flight and called out desperately, "Naomi, wait! You misunderstood!"

They were words spoken too late; Naomi had vanished behind the closed bedroom door on the second floor. Edward stood exacerbated at the bottom of the winding staircase.

Dare I attempt to repair the damage? He stroked Heidi and readily concluded—not under these conditions. He returned Rusty and Heidi to the basket by the kitchen stove.

With a quick snatch of his tweed overcoat from the coat rack, Edward left the mansion in a state of total frustration to return to his home, Brachney Hall. With his hands tucked in his pockets, he attacked the cobblestones with intermittent kicks and mumbled self-depreciating comments with each step. A disagreement with Naomi couldn't have occurred at a worse time. His debonair nephew would be arriving soon and Edward's confidence in his relationship with Naomi was still wavering. Although Edward and Naomi, had declared their love for each other, and he adored his nephew,

Edward still felt the threatening presence of Naomi's first love.

Chapter III

"The Box"

His purposes will ripen fast,
Unfolding every hour;
The bud may have a bitter taste,
But sweet will be the flower.

—William Cowper

Eloise waited fearfully at her home, the caretaker's cottage for McDonnally Manor. Guillaume would arrive shortly, returning from an errand to the village with his father. Her unsteady hand placed a letter back in its envelope, then safely into her handkerchief box. She shook her head knowing Trina was determined to win Guillaume back. Eloise had thought of the young woman as a daughter, but was convinced that the relationship was impossible; Guillaume would never consent to live in Paris as Trina had hoped. His wanderlust would take him to the ends of the earth leaving Trina's dogged efforts in vain. Eloise had failed to reply to either of her letters, knowing she could offer no encouragement.

The apprehensive mother took her place in the rocker on the tiny white washed porch and sat tensely with her knitting needles and a pink ball of yarn in her lap. She rocked erratically in the caned rocker, watching the sun slip toward the horizon. She prayed her son would forgive her. The sound of hooves on the cobblestones alerted her that the old shire pulling the cart would appear momentarily.

The overwhelming dread of the meeting with Guillaume was curbed by her wish to have the matter out in the open. Hopefully, he could clear his name with the poor Allison, now fretting needlessly, upstairs in the manor house.

Seeing his mother, now sitting with her hands covering her downcast face, Guillaume jumped from the wagon and rushed to her side.

"Mother, what is the matter? Mother, it's... it's not Allison!" Guillaume's first and foremost concern, if not obsession. The question took his mother off guard as she fell back in the rocker, sobbing into her apron.

"Mother, what has happened to her? Tell me, Mother!" the distraught son insisted. His father, Albert, dropped the grain sacks from the wagon and rushed to his wife's side.

"Eloise, dear, what is wrong?"

"Allison..." was the only word capable of passing through her lips, before Guillaume shot toward the mansion in a full sprint. He hurdled the flower beds and the concrete bench. He flung open the door to the back hall and let out a desperate call, "Allison!" He darted to the parlor, then across the hall to the study to call once again, "Allison where are you?"

Believing the worst, he scaled the staircase full speed when his right foot made unfortunate contact with the tapestry rug in the hall. Sliding out of control, Guillaume became airborne. He flew past the McDonnally portraits, headlong into a small oak table on the adjacent wall, displaying the marble bust of Hiram's great Grandfather Geoffrey McDonnally. The upended art piece toppled from the table and landed with a thud on Guillaume's back which precipitated a low groan from its victim.

Fortunately, Naomi was just stepping from the bedroom, two doors down, blotting her eyes with her handkerchief when she caught sight of the familiar heap on the corridor floor. Naomi, forgetting her troubles, fled to the scene and dropped down by the young suitor.

"Oh, Guillaume, are you badly hurt?" She lifted Geoffrey from Guillaume's back and set it on the floor next to her.

The injured party was oblivious to her inquiry. "Allison, where is Allison?" he implored with an aching breath.

"In the room, down the hall."

"Oh, dear God," he muttered, struggling to all fours. "My poor Allison, my darling," he uttered between breaths.

"Guillaume, I don't think that you should try to stand," Naomi counseled as he struggled to lift himself. Naomi quickly assisted supporting his left elbow, as he slowly rose to his feet.

"I must see her," he beckoned.

"Are you sure, Guillaume? I think that you need to sit for a spell and get your bearings," Naomi suggested sympathetically.

"I'm fine...please, humor me... and help me, please...I must see her." He held his right hand on his hip, crouching with the stance of an elderly man in need of a cane. Naomi placed his left arm over her shoulder and aided the anxious man to the bedroom where Allison lay on the bed sulking scornfully. When the hobbling couple reached their destination, Naomi knocked, reached for the glass door knob and turned it slowly trying to maintain her balance. The door creaked open revealing the crumpled figure leaning heavily on Naomi, now straining under the weight of the accident victim.

Dazed, Guillaume took one look at Allison, and half-smiled, then reported, "I think I'm going to be sick," as his eyes rolled back.

"Not in my room! How disgusting!" The ailing guest keeled over, slipping from Naomi's grip around his waist.

"Allison! Will *you* please help me?" Naomi demanded. Allison slid out from beneath the chenille coverlet to join her mother. The two gently rolled Guillaume to his side. A small, black velvet box fell from his upper pocket, landing inches from the oak threshold. The fallen object captured the immediate attention of both curious women as was apparent by their immediate eye contact with one another. Naomi initiated the first move to recover the box when Allison's hand fell on her mother's simultaneously. Their eyes met once again.

"Is that a ring box?" Allison asked in a hushed tone.

"I...I would say so, but we have more important matters at hand." Naomi placed the box on the floor and ran her hand across Guillaume's forehead and loosened his collar. She lifted his wrist to check his pulse. "Yes, he's fine, he has passed out, he'll wake in a moment," Naomi insisted.

"But Mummy, it's a ring box. Do you know what this could mean? Guillaume had it in his pocket."

"Yes...I know."

"Do you think that it's... well, I mean, one could almost assume..." she hesitated as she tucked her skirt around her, kneeling on the floor. "Oh, he has to be all right. My perfect Guillaume, you wonderful man," Allison doted, observing the limp body next to her and the intriguing box.

Naomi looked to Guillaume, then picked up the box and turned it over methodically, looking for the proper orientation to lift the lid.

"Mummy, open it! I can't bear the suspense!" she whispered, entranced by the case that her mother held. "Maybe we could just peek at it... It may be a ring for himself."

"Allison!"

"All right then, I shan't look at it... you take a quick peek. There's no harm in looking. Why it may even be damaged from the fall. We should probably check."

"I doubt that it was damaged... but you never know." Naomi's unleashed curiosity overcame her better judgment as it did that regretful afternoon on the third floor when she trespassed into Hiram's late mother's room. Since that day, she suffered with the torment of silence with her discovery of a letter which revealed the kidnapping of Hiram's missing twin.

"Perhaps...just one quick look."

Allison gently shielded her intended's closed eyes with her cupped hands. The tension increased while her mother cracked the tiny hinged lid.

"Hurry, Mother! I think he's coming to."

Naomi's wide-eyed gasp sent Allison into an uncontrolled frenzy, snatching the opened box from her mother's weakened fingers. Gawking at the jeweled elegance, Allison's mouth dropped as her eyes caressed the glimmering diamond engagement ring. The center stone was a round three carat setting encircled by a ring of tiny emeralds; the band was scrolled gold. The shock of the extravagant gem cushioned within the white silk pillow foundation of the black velvet case left both women speechless.

With the stirring of the recovering young man, Allison quickly closed the lid and returned it carefully to Guillaume's vest pocket. His sapphire eyes gradually appeared to greet the smiles of Naomi and daughter.

"Guillaume, how are you feeling," Naomi asked innocently.

"I think I'm experiencing a deja vous. Remember when we first met, Mrs. McDonnally?"

"Yes, Guillaume, you were waking from a horrid blow to your head from those unconscionable thieves."

He turned to Allison and selflessly inquired, "Allison, should you be out of bed? You should conserve your strength." He rubbed his forehead and asked, "If I may be so bold ...as to inquire... I don't want to be impertinent, but what ails you?"

"Nothing, my dear sweet Guillaume, nothing at all," she whispered running her finger across his forehead to brush the hair from his eyes. Thoughts of Guillaume's alleged engagement floated like unwanted ghosts from the room, driven away by the promising jewel resting next to his heart.

Naomi's tongue pressed the inside of her cheek while her green eyes narrowed witnessing the remarkable modification in her daughter's attitude. Guillaume soaked up the lovely girl's praises like an enormous sponge, his ego expanding with her every word.

"Now my poor darling, I think it would be wise to help you to the bed. There you can rest comfortably. Don't you agree, mother?"

"Of course," Naomi complied with a Cheshire grin, helping the lovesick patient across the room to recuperate.

"There, how's that, Guillaume?" Allison inquired with soft spoken drama.

"Oh, fine, my dear Allison, thank you. If you don't mind, I could rest here for a few minutes 'til I get my wits about me.

"Certainly." The accommodating nursemaid puffed the pillows behind his square shoulders.

Naomi gave the couple a second look and opened the door a tad wider, then excused herself to fetch a glass of water from the pantry, for the pathetic patient. With each step down the winding oak staircase, disturbing thoughts of the exquisite ring crept into her mind. The ring was beautiful, but too beautiful, too extravagant for a groom of Guillaume's status. He was by no means wealthy and most assuredly in no position to present a token of that caliber to her daughter.

She took a deep breath as she stepped into the pantry to retrieve a glass from the cupboard. She filled it from the metal pitcher next to a jar of fresh biscuits that Eloise baked that morning. Naomi unconsciously removed the lid, savored the tantalizing scent of ginger and chose one. She lowered herself into the chair next to the table and nibbled the tasty find. Lost in the mystery, she loosened her grip on the glass, sliding her fingers aimlessly around its perimeter. She stopped chewing when the discomforting thought occurred to her that Guillaume may have taken a loan for the ring, a large loan, a debt that would take many years to repay.

Does he believe that Allison would demand such an outlandish ring? Surely, she hasn't said anything to give him that impression. She finished the last bite followed by a sip of water, when Albert, father of the not so frugal groom entered the kitchen.

"Good day Mum...have you seen my son?"

"Oh yes, he's upstairs in Allison's bed... I mean in Allison's room in bed," Naomi struggled to correct her misleading reply. Albert cocked his head and frowned, waiting for a more acceptable answer.

"Well, you see Mr. Zigmann; I was on my way to take him this glass of water." Holding the glass before her, she realized her credibility was dwindling; Albert had arrived just in time to see her drinking from it. The sixty year old man, clad in trousers and pinstripe shirt placed a thumb under each of his leather suspenders and flipped them against his chest with apparent dissatisfaction with Naomi's explanation.

"Mum...might I ask you again? Where is Guillaume?"

"Now Albert, it is not all as you may imagine. You see, Guillaume took a fall...I mean to say that he slipped on the rug."

"What?"

"Oh, he's quite all right. You're familiar with the one in the hall at the top of the stairs? The rug that is."

"Yes..."

"Well, to make a long tale short," she began to giggle uncomfortably. "I mean a short story long, no...a long story short," she gave a quick headshake, "Guillaume is recovering upstairs...I'm sure he'd be delighted to see you," she half-heartedly suggested.

Observing Albert's impatience and unfavorable mood, Naomi prayed silently that her starry-eyed daughter would not be found in the arms of Albert's missing offspring. The perturbed father nodded and headed to the second floor, with Naomi not far behind.

"I understand that you and Mr. Dugan will be providing the musical entertainment for the celebration," Naomi tried to regain the angered father's favor.

"Yes," was all that he said.

Much to their surprise, Albert's mission ended when he found the two lovebirds conversing quietly, seated on the top step with Allison snuggling under Guillaume's arm. With Albert's looming presence, Allison jumped to her feet and straightened her woolen skirt and timidly smoothed the lace edging on each cuff of her silk blouse.

"Well, I see you both have apparently recovered. Excuse us Miss O'Connor, but Guillaume's mother would like a word with him." Allison motioned for the son to go with his father, glowing with approval, imagining Albert as her future father-in-law. She stood respectfully and sent an encouraging wink to her mother. Naomi immediately checked her daughter's finger for the ring, relieved to find that it was not displayed, as yet.

"Join me in the kitchen won't you Allison, Eloise made fresh gingersnaps."

"Certainly, Mother...if you care to speak with me later, Guillaume, I'll be here at the manor for the remainder of the evening, remember I am saving all my dances for you."

"Yes, Allison —" his comments ended by a helpful tug from his father.

"Let's go, son, your mother is waiting."

The love struck couple exchanged promising glances as they were led away by their parents. The two women continued to the kitchen, while Albert and Guillaume returned to the cottage where Eloise sat drained from the ordeal.

Before Guillaume's foot hit the threshold, Albert reprimanded, "Son, what right have you to put your mother, this kind, generous always loving woman, in such a despicable situation?" Guillaume squinted slightly at his father and then turned to his mother filled with regret.

"Oh, Mother, did I worry you? I left like a bat out of— pardon me, Mother. Don't fret, Allison is fine and my injuries are minimal. I really am physically fine."

Albert interrupted, "Now see here, young man, the only injuries we're discussing right now are those that your dear mother suffered because *you* put her in an embarrassing situation! She shouldn't have had to be the one to inform Miss O'Connor of your engagement to Trina."

"What! Mother, you told Allison about Trina?" Guilluame inadvertently clutched his mother's shoulders. Eloise's fearful eyes welled up.

"Here, here! Unhand that woman! She's your beloved mother," Albert demanded.

"Sorry, Mother." Guillaume sat down silently next to his mother and in a much calmer voice proceeded with the questioning, "Why would you tell her?"

Albert defensively stepped in, "Don't be interrogating your mother; the details are of no interest. I demand that you apologize to your Mother this instant!"

"I just did, Father."

"Don't be insolent! You should have told Miss O'Connor months ago."

"But Father, I've known Allison only a few weeks."

"I don't care if you have known her only a few days! Secrets are trouble. Now, apologize!"

Guillaume turned from his father's scarlet face to his solemn mother and humbly addressed her, "Mother, I am truly sorry. I never meant to put you in an uncomfortable position, but how exactly did this happen?"

"Guillaume!" his father shouted.

"Is Allison awfully angry with you?" Eloise asked blotting her nose with her handkerchief.

"On the contrary, she was quite pleased to see me," Guillaume announced proudly.

"I don't understand, however, Naomi did try to reason with her," Eloise pondered, but considered the fickleness common to women of Allison's age. "I realize that you are an adult and capable of making your own decisions, but as your mother, I must say that I believe that you are playing with fire."

"Trina is part of the past, gone forever. Thanks to Naomi, my future mother-in-law's motherly advice, we need not be concerned about the subject any further," Guillaume satisfactorily deducted as he leaned over to hug his skeptical mother.

The weight of the world was lifted from Eloise's shoulders only to be replaced by the fear that Trina would not relent to her son's decision to end the relationship. Albert shook his head at a loss to the mystery of women and young love.

Chapter IV

"The Ring"

Jewels are baubles;
'tis a sin
To care for such unfruitful things;—
One good-sized diamond in a pin,—
Some, *not so large*, in rings,
A ruby, and a pearl, or so,
Will do for me;—I laugh at show.

—Oliver Wendell Holmes

Edward peered out across the moors, re-evaluating his status with Naomi.

Well then, I may not have chosen the proper place, as yet, but I have the ring. At least, I hope Guillaume remembered to pick it up from the shipping office. Edward pulled on his coat to return to McDonnally Manor to clear up the misunderstanding with Naomi. With the crisp autumn winds curling around his bare neck, he flipped up his collar and quickened his pace.

In the mansion, Naomi and daughter chatted quietly over tea and the tasty treat. Within fifteen seconds, the topic of the sacred gem resurfaced.

"Mummy, don't you think that the stone is awfully large? I don't mean to appear ungrateful, but it could be easily mistaken for a piece that the queen would don for tea. It *is* extraordinary."

"Baby, extraordinary is hardly the adjective that one would choose to describe it. It's incredible." Allison detected her mother's disturbed expression.

"What's wrong, Mummy? Don't you think that I'm worthy of such a gift? Not that I have a great need or desire for such an outlandish engagement ring," she added modestly, lowering her head.

"I'm very glad to hear you say that Allison. I know that you enjoy the finer luxuries, but you *are* sensible, for the most part."

"Yes, Mummy. I must say that I am concerned about the resources that Guillaume extinguished to pay for it. After all, as his future wife and financial partner, it will be my responsibility to assist in maintaining the household finances," Allison added with an air of maturity.

"Maybe Guillaume has a trust fund or inheritance or he may have actually inherited the—" Naomi stopped short.

The conversation was diverted when the doorknocker's rapping sounded through the main hall. Naomi left Allison to enjoy the last biscuit, to peek through the sidelight. She found Edward casually waiting with his hands tucked in his pockets and staring blankly at the empty concrete planters in the portal. Naomi opened the door to greet Edward with an open mind and grateful heart.

"Hello, Edward."

"Hello."

"Would you like to come in?"

"Oh, I thought that we might take a stroll."

"Certainly, I'll get my cape." Naomi left the door ajar and pulled the new burgundy cape from the coat hook. Allison had bought it for her in London as a "travel present". "Baby, Edward and I are stepping out for a bit," she called.

"Enjoy the fresh air!"

"We will," Edward replied as he closed the heavy door behind Naomi.

Naomi fastened the cape then shot an amorous smile up to her suitor who stood a good head taller than her. They wandered across the cobblestone drive to the meadow when Edward commented, "It's sweet that you still call her 'baby'."

"She'll always be my baby, even when she's sixty."

"How's she doing Naomi? She seems in much better spirits since she and Guillaume got together."

"Oh, yes, she's fine now...I guess."

"I'm sorry that I upset you, Naomi."

"I hope you aren't angry with me, Edward. I never meant to run away. I'm more appreciative than you could ever imagine for the life you have given Allison and me."

"Oh Naomi, you know that you're my magic square. I couldn't possibly be angry with you. This was our first lover's—our first spat, Naomi," he assured.

"What did you call me?"

"Naomi."

"No before that; something about a square."

"My magic square."

"Edward, perhaps I am missing something, but what is a magic square?"

"Here, I'll show you. I need a twig."

A twig?

After discarding several small twigs, Edward selected a longer stick, a half inch in diameter and a foot in length.

What are you doing?

"This will do nicely," he held up the stick swinging it mischievously. Naomi took a step back from the weapon wielding avenger.

"What are you going to do with that, Edward?" Naomi asked cautiously.

"I'm going to use it as a drawing implement, silly woman," he explained as he knelt down to a dusty, vacant area along side of the road.

"Oh?" she watched skeptically.

Edward proceeded to sketch a square a foot wide in the dust and then divided it into nine equal boxes. Naomi watched curiously as Edward inscribed each box with a different numeral.

"There it is, the magic square," Edward announced proudly. Naomi's auburn locks bounced in the breeze as she bent over to examine the diagram at her feet.

$$6 \quad 7 \quad 2$$
$$1 \quad 5 \quad 9$$
$$8 \quad 3 \quad 4$$

"That's lovely Edward, but what is its purpose?"

"That's you, the magic square. You see, it's perfect from every angle."

"It is?"

"Of course it is. Add the top row of numbers."

"The sum is fifteen."

"Now, add the middle and the bottom rows."

"Fifteen again, that's amazing, Edward."

"That's only the beginning. Now add the columns."

"Unbelievable, Edward."

"Now would you venture, to add them diagonally?" Edward teased.

"No doubt, fifteen. Edward you are a genius. How did you ever derive at this?"

"It was simple; I consulted with an ancient Chinese scholar."

"And when did this alleged meeting occur?" Naomi gave a sideways glance.

"About three thousand years ago."

"Oh, Edward," she tapped his shoulder playfully. "It is such a strange phenomenon."

"As are you, Naomi McDonnally. Miraculously perfect from every angle, in all that you are and all that you do. You are my magic square."

Naomi's guilt immediately surfaced, "You may have second thoughts about your term of endearment after I explain what Allison and I have done."

"And what despicable crime have you and your lovely daughter committed?" he inquired, offering her his right arm. As they entered the meadow, Naomi sighed not knowing quite where to begin.

"Edward, I have to confess. Allison and I have violated Guillaume's privacy."

"How so?"

Naomi continued tautly, "Earlier today, Guillaume had an accident. He slipped and Geoffrey's head knocked him unconscious and we picked up the box. I knew that I shan't open it, much less have shown it to Allison... I have failed as a mother. I'm definitely not a shining example, by any means."

"Geoffrey's head?"

"Yes, the bust in the hall upstairs, it fell on him."

"Was he hurt? Edward asked with genuine concern.

"No, just stunned."

"And you took his box? What box?"

"Guillaume's box."

Edward continued extracting information, like pulling good teeth.

"Was this Guillaume's strong box or a private chest?"

"Don't be ridiculous Edward. I would never open a box with personal—" She stopped dead in her tracks. *Yes, I would, not a month ago when I opened Amanda's trunk.*

"Edward, it was a ring box. It fell from his pocket."

"A what?" Edward snapped.

"Well, you need not be so surprised, we all knew that Allison and Guillaume were headed for the altar."

"Did Guillaume give you permission to look at it?" Edward asked with apparent anxiety.

"No, like I said, he was unconscious when I peeked in at it."

Edward closed his eyes with disappointment, "You did?"

"Allison did as well," Naomi defended. "Oh, Edward, it was beautiful."

"Did you really think so?" Edward smiled, encouraged.

"Oh yes, but it is too much."

"You mean too dear?"

"Too dear? It must have cost a fortune! And too big, too elaborate, just too much. Allison is really not the type to wear such an ostentatious piece."

"Allison?"

"Yes, Edward, don't you understand? It is an engagement ring for Allison."

"I see. So, Naomi, you think that it's well... too much for a girl of her age?"

"Most definitely. Frankly, I don't know anyone who would wear such a ring. It really belongs in a showcase, not on someone's finger. It's just too much. My heart goes out to Guillaume; the poor young man must have spent a fortune on it. Maybe you should talk to him. You could advise him."

"Oh, trust me, I *will* talk to him, that is certain," Edward clenched his teeth, tightening his jaw.

"I can't imagine what can be done, Edward. Allison has already seen it. He can't return it now. I just don't know," Naomi spoke sympathetically.

"I will see what I can do," Edward choked out the words.

"My Edward, you seem very upset."

"Upset, no that's doesn't begin to describe how I feel," he muttered as they turned to head back to the mansion.

"Edward?"

"I don't understand this younger generation. Naomi, if you see Guillaume, please ask him, to pay me a call at Brachney Hall, tomorrow."

"Of course, Edward. Do you know what time Hiram is expected to arrive?"

"Not really, Eloise seems to have everything under control for the celebration. Would you care to join me for supper at the inn? Allison is welcome too," he added struggling to cloak his depression.

"That would be fine, Edward."

"Very, well then, I will return for you at five." He leaned over and kissed her sweetly, forcing a smile and hastening her in out of the cold before he left for Brachney Hall. He turned and waved, "See you soon, love!"

Now, what am I going to do? She thinks it's for Allison. What's worse, she hates it, he shook his head in defeat.

Naomi waved, shivered in her cape and rushed inside.

Chapter V

"Sticky Wicket"

No man complaining,
No other disdaining,
For loss or for gaining,
But fellows or friends to be.
No grudge remaining,
No work refraining,
Nor help restraining,
But lovingly to agree.

—Nicholas Udall

Guillaume arrived at Brachney Hall the next day. Edward greeted him at the door.

"Good morning, sir. Here's the ring. Sorry that I didn't deliver it yesterday, but I had a small mishap. A slight injury," Guillaume explained handing the ring box to Edward. Edward took the box, opened the lid and held it before him, examining it as he spoke, in a controlled low tone.

"Yes, a small mishap. Guillaume we are in a bit of a sticky wicket." Edward shook his head with closed eyes, still having trouble accepting the situation.

"How so, sir?"

"Unfortunately, during your acrobatic display with Grandfather McDonnally's bust, Naomi's engagement ring escaped from your pocket. Not only that, it found its way into the hands of *your intended* and mine."

"Oh, no! Mrs. McDonnally saw the ring?"

"Yes, as did Allison."

"Oh sir, I'm so sorry. I don't know what I can say," Guillaume lowered his head remorsefully.

"Guillaume, you may drop the formality and call me Edward."

"Yes, sir...I mean Edward." Guillaume looked up hopefully and asked, "Did Mrs. McDonnally like the ring?"

"She didn't believe that it was for her."

"For whom then, sir?"

"For Allison, of course."

"But why would she think that you would purchase an engagement ring for her daughter?"

Edward stared blankly at the innocent face of his clueless young friend. Edward got up and rubbed his head with both hands as he began pacing the floor. He stopped, cast an *I don't believe that I am hearing this* look toward his seated young friend and then addressed him seriously. "Guillaume, how badly were you injured in the fall?"

"Sir? I mean, Edward?"

"Think man, think!" Edward's stress began to take hold. "Naturally, Naomi and Allison assumed that the ring case that fell from *your waistcoat* pocket held a ring that *you* chose for Allison."

"Allison knows that I could never afford a ring like that. She had to have known that it was not for her," Guillaume defended himself.

"Then why was it in your pocket?" Edward challenged.

"Sir?" Guillaume questioned in the pandemonium. "Sir, have you forgotten? You asked me to pick it up for you at the shipping office." Guillaume cautiously attempted to clear up the matter.

"Guillaume, yes, of course I know that. I was attempting to explain their point of view." Edward walked a few steps away and then turned. "Sorry... this is a frustrating situation for all of us. The point is, Allison believes that the ring will be hers when you propose."

Guillaume flew from his chair "Oh, no...that will never do! Then I won't propose." Guillaume clutched the back of the chair. "You're absolutely right. Let's tell them the truth."

"Have you lost your mind?"

"No sir. I just thought that, good sports that they are, they would understand and we'd all have a jolly good laugh over it," Guillaume rationalized.

"Guillaume, we're not dealing with a mix up over a box of sweets. You are not thinking clearly.

We have two very sensitive women to deal with; we have to consider their feelings. We *do* have to live with them the rest of our lives. We have to act prudently," Edward explained, his patience wearing thin. "Do you want to be the one to tell Allison that the exquisite ring that she adores, according to Naomi, is intended for her mother... and that she'll be lucky to receive a modest token one tenth the value?"

"Now, hold on! I can certainly provide something a little better than that."

"I don't think so Guillaume...in fact, I'm sure of it."

"Is it that valuable?" Guillaume returned to the chair.

Edward nodded.

"Sir, we could tell them that yours is bogus, you know, an imitation...cut glass." As Edward's eyes narrowed with the comment, Guillaume amended his statement, "Perhaps, an expertly produced replica?"

"And how do you think Naomi is going to feel about me, a man of significant means, purchasing a counterfeit, oversized, ostentatious, monstrosity that she can't imagine anyone reputable wearing, for her engagement?"

"What! How dare she criticize my engagement ring."

"Guillaume, concentrate. It's not *your* engagement ring."

"Right... Naomi really said that?"

"Well, not exactly, she mentioned that it was *very* large with a hint of negativity."

"Maybe she was jealous. Sour grapes, you know."

"No, Naomi has always been honest about her feelings. She didn't say much. She didn't want to criticize *your* choice; you know she thinks the world of you, Guillaume."

"And I her...So let me analyze this situation. Hmm? Allison is thrilled with the prospect of getting the ring in question and Naomi despises it. I guess I'll have to buy it from you... on a payment plan of sorts."

"No, Guillaume, I don't mean to offend you, but I don't think that it would be in your best interest to invest two years of your future salary on an engagement ring."

"Two years! Six months is debilitating enough."

"Six months? Have you already purchased a ring for Allison?" Edward queried with a glimmer of hope.

"Not exactly."

"Why didn't you tell me that you were already in the process of buying her a ring? This adds a new twist to the matter, Guillaume."

"Not really, sir. The ring wasn't for Allison," Guillaume added under his breath.

"What did you say? Speak up." Edward's frustration returned.

"The ring was not for Allison."

"Not for Allison? Guillaume what have you done? You are not betrothed to someone else are you?"

"No, no this was a long time ago," Guillaume reassured him with an insincere smile.

"That's a relief. If I might ask, exactly how long ago? Guillaume you are only twenty-three." The defendant gulped and remained silently cornered. "Guillaume...I realize this is a personal question, but I am getting the impression that this little matter of the ring is even more complex than I thought."

"Less than six months ago...sir... Edward."

"Only a few months before you arrived at McDonnally Manor?" Edward asked with fatherly concern.

"Yes, sir...but it's over with Trina. I love Allison now. I want her to be my wife, but she refuses to accept it." Guillaume explained, now pacing aimlessly.

"Guillaume, get a hold of yourself. Of course, she accepts it or she wouldn't be so excited about the ring."

"No, sir, not Allison, Trina. She won't let me go. I told her it was over when I left Paris, but she's wearing the ring and insists that it's only a matter of time before I'll come back to her. She's telling everyone that I took leave for a short visit with my parents. I'm not going back, Edward...and she's been threatening to come here."Edward sat down and pondered both situations.

"Edward, about the ring, why don't you return it to the Craig Jewelry Store, that's all you can do? Besides, neither one of them should have been taking unauthorized liberties with the box. Then you can purchase another ring, one that's a little less...I'll accompany you," Guillaume suggested cheerily.

"That's a generous thought Guillaume; however, that's impossible. The Craigs have a strict policy about returns on special orders with large stones."

Edward, with his hands on the back of the chair, leaned toward Guillaume. "Don't you believe that Trina, will retreat once she finds that you are keeping company with Allison?"

"Probably not, sir. She's a fighter."

"Allison isn't exactly timid either, Guillaume. Not that a duel is the answer."

"Sorry about the ring, sir."

"It was an accident. I guess all things happen for a reason. I would have given Naomi the ring and she would have probably worn it, despising it every second." The two men looked empathetically at each other, entrenched in the unresolved dilemma.

"This is terrible, Edward...maybe we should consult with a higher authority."

"Yes, a prayer right now couldn't hurt."

"With no disrespect, sir, I was actually referring to my father. He's been around longer than either one of us. He knows how to handle his women," Guillaume proudly reported.

"His women?" Edward smiled skeptically.

"Well, he's happily married to Mother and rarely upsets her."

"I don't know, Guillaume. Although I am sure Albert could offer some good advice, I don't believe that we should get anyone else involved."

"You are probably right. Father is a stickler for the truth; he doesn't approve of secrets. He says they're trouble."

"Guillaume, I don't like this any more than you do. Let's sleep on it. We'll discuss it tomorrow; I think that we have exhausted the possibilities for now. Until we come up with a suitable resolution, please do not discuss anything about this with

anyone else, especially not with Allison or Naomi."
Edward opened the door, turning for confirmation.
"You need not worry about that; I wouldn't
touch that beehive, if my life depended on it...well it
probably does, now that I think about it." Guillaume outstretched his hand, "It's a pact; my lips
are sealed," Guillaume assured with a flair for the
dramatic. Edward shook his hand in treaty.

"Good afternoon Guillaume. I'm certain that
it will all work out," Edward reassured lamely.

"Good afternoon, sir." Guillaume hurried off
to the cottage behind McDonnally Manor and retired to the kitchen, when he spotted his parents
walking across the meadow from Harriet and Joseph Dugan's home. They were returning from a
scheduled visit to showoff the dachshund puppy
which they had purchased earlier from Mrs. Dugan.
Guillaume waved from the window as they approached. Guillaume greeted his parents as they
drew closer to the cottage.

"How was your visit with the Dugans?"

"Quite nice, thank you, son. Harriet barely
recognized our little Rusty. He's so much larger
now, and longer. She says he takes after his father,
a handsome sire," Eloise smiled with pride as she
entered the door.

"And Father, how's Mr. Dugan, these days?
Does he still have that ornery old mule?"

"Joseph is Joseph. Never changes much and
he still has Jock," Albert added while hanging
Eloise's coat on the peg next to his. "Joseph keeps
you smiling with those tales he hears from Wiggins."

Eloise muttered, "Nothing, you'd dare repeat.
I don't know why he doesn't tend to his butchering

and leave the story telling to the vicar; at least his are suitable for God fearing people." Eloise tucked her puppy in the small basket by the fireplace and covered it with a tiny blue coverlet that she had knitted.

"How was your chat with Mr. McDonnally, son?" Albert queried. "Did you remember to give him the ring?" Albert's tone emulated his usual lack of confidence in his forgetful offspring.

Eloise's head shot up with newfound curiosity and a look of betrayal, scowling at her husband, for withholding information. She questioned Albert before Guillaume had a chance to respond. "What ring, Albert?"

Guillaume stood behind his mother, frantically shaking his head, alerting his father to withdraw from any further commentary on the subject. Observing his son, nearing fits of conniptions, Albert, uncomfortably, but loyally, relented to a recovery plan.

"Did I say ring? I meant—" he faltered.

Before he initiated a revision, his elated wife cut in, "A ring for Naomi...a real engagement ring? I knew he'd ask her to marry him, again!"

Albert angrily searched his disturbed son's face for guidance, for the first time in his life. Eloise turned to Guillaume as well, for confirmation of her supposition. Guillaume helplessly faced his parents, the two people who taught him that honesty was everything; that lies, even little white ones were unacceptable. For the moment, the Zigmann family stood silent, all three unsure of what was to follow. Guillaume reached for the rocking chair behind him and moved slowly back to it and took a seat without a word.

Eloise realized that once again, she had entered forbidden territory. She looked to her silent husband and feebly invited, "Anyone care for tea?" Her two men nodded. Eloise placed the kettle on the stove and retrieved the tea jar from the cupboard. She called out with assurance, "Don't worry, my lips are sealed. I shan't breathe a word of this to Mrs. McDonnally."

Guillaume noted the irony that she had chosen the same phrase he had promised with earlier. *I guess I am definitely my mother's son.* He called back, "I would appreciate it!" His father folded his arms, wearily.

Within a few minutes, the little family was sipping tea from Eloise's earthenware cups; the room was void of conversation. Guillaume peered into the tiny tea pool of his cup, sinking deeper into depression with the realization that two more members had been added to the cataclysmic chaos of "The Ring." He cringed with thoughts of his future confrontation with Edward, imagining Edward's disappointment as he lamely attempted to explain his innocence.

Eloise sat across from her son, nearly bursting with curiosity. She felt that she would most certainly perish within the hour if she was denied the details of the jewel and the circumstances surrounding it. Eloise held back, hoping her son would rescue her from the grips of unbearable ignorance and reveal another tidbit to revive her. However, he said nothing. Albert, who found the household drama vexing, decided to bring it all to an end.

"Eloise, the truth is that Edward McDonnally's business is Edward McDonnally's. Not the Zigmanns'." With this remark, she woefully took her empty cup to the kitchen, mumbling, "Yes, Albert." Guillaume watched his mother pass, relieved that her knowledge would not further complicate matters, as long as she kept her promise to remain silent.

Chapter VI

"The Potter"

And all my days are trances,
And all my nightly dreams
Are where thy dark eye glances,
And where thy footstep gleams—

—Edgar Allen Poe

After twenty-four hours, Hiram relented to his haunted conscience and returned to visit with the woman at the Autumn Art Exposition.

"Hello."

"Hello."

"Pleasant day for the art exposition," Hiram commented.

"Yes," the woman replied, with her gray eyes downcast. "Is there anything in particular that you are looking for?"

"Well..." Hiram quickly surveyed the pieces when a small child, tugging on her mother's hand, pointed at one of the smaller oils displayed towards the front.

"Look, Mummy, a cow like Uncle Sean's!"

"No, Kathryn, that is not a cow, it is a dog... well, perhaps not. I'm not certain what it is."

"Excuse me, but I couldn't help overhearing the conversation that you were having with your lovely daughter. She is your daughter, is she not?" Hiram inquired.

"Why yes, but..."

"I was certain of it. She has your intriguing eyes and rich hair coloring."

"Do you think so, sir?" the mother smiled modestly. The artist rolled her eyes.

"Definitely, and how creatively observant you both are. This piece is neither cow nor dog, but a product of the talented artist to test the strengths of the imagination of the viewer. You have success-fully passed the test. You both share creative gen-ius and should possibly consider taking up the arts as well. Have you ever critiqued professionally?"

"Why no, sir."

"I'm surprised. Food for thought. Good day, Madame."

"Good day, sir." The woman left the exhibit smiling proudly and continued on to the next exhibit.

Meanwhile, the artist of the controversial piece sat dumbfounded, staring at the handsome defender in awe, as he waved to the satiated mother and child. Hiram turned back to the exhibit and moved closer to a framed portrait of an elderly woman, knitting. With folded arms, he stroked his beard as he studied it with seemingly no acknowledgement to the prior incident. He took particular interest in the artist's signature. *Elizabeth, how beautiful,* he thought.

The embarrassed artist was preoccupied as well, but with her interest centralized on him, the stranger dressed in the finest attire.

A gentleman, a member of the upper echelon. Why would he defend my paintings? She gave him another once over. *Enough is enough,* she felt that it was time to put an end to this charade. It was no longer necessary for him to endure his apparent torture in humoring her with his attention to her less than professional talent.

"I appreciate your efforts but I am certain a man of your situation has a great deal of pressing engagements. You need not waste your time observing pieces unworthy of adorning the walls of your residence. I am not so foolish to believe that my paintings are of the caliber of which you are accustomed. Unless, of course, you take some strange pleasure in rescuing failing merchants from public scrutiny."

Hiram's dark eyes penetrated the gray gaze of the proud woman, who felt disarmed with their gentleness and his silence. She felt herself slipping into some inescapable trance, sealing out the rest of the world. She was drawn back to reality when his eyes dropped from hers, and fell to her hand clenching a unique coffee cup.

"Allow me to introduce myself, Hiram McDonnally," he removed his hat and bowed slightly from the waist.

His handsome raven hair drew her immediate attention. *Naturally, display the hair as well. A McDonnally of the McDonnallys.*

"Elizabeth. Of course, you already knew that."

He ignored her sarcasm and continued, "That's an interesting piece of artwork, Elizabeth," he remarked as Elizabeth looked down to the point of his focus.

My hand?

"That's an interesting vessel, you have there."

Elizabeth looked down at the piece of pottery, "Seems to be the public consensus."

"I am not surprised that others share my opinion. It is quite unique."

"Yes, I've had close to a dozen customers inquire about this cup."

Hiram moved in closer to take a better look. Elizabeth held it up and ran her finger around the rim as she described it in a mock dreamy tone. "Notice the smooth lines, the delicate way in which the artist has incorporated the theme in the handle...observe the..." She broke into what Hiram found to be a delightful bout of giggling. He laughed with her, enchanted by her sweet childlike response.

"Excuse me," she caught her breath, "But this silly cup has upstaged my entire exhibit. Maybe I should frame it and sell it."

"May I?" Elizabeth surrendered the cup. "How *did* you acquire it?"

"I decided that after an hour on the pottery wheel at Mrs. Divine's School for Girls, I should probably keep it.

"You are the creator of this extraordinary piece?" Hiram asked as he carefully examined the empty cup stained with her morning coffee ration.

"Surprised? Does it not look like the rest of my masterpieces?" she smiled from the corner of her mouth as she spread her arms behind a pair of paintings. One depicted a windmill set solely on a hill with a Dutch girl in the foreground, the other of a lone boat beached on the sand of an inlet beneath snowcapped mountains.

"In all seriousness, this is quite professional, I am impressed," Hiram confessed.

"Oh... and these are not?" she teased.

Hiram sought her forgiveness, "I beg your pardon...I think that perhaps, you should consider pottery works as a lucrative profession."

"My, my, no truer words were spoken ...by a man who convinced a stranger that she should seek employment in the business of art critiquing; her five year old daughter as well, a dual employment opportunity!" she countered. "Maybe you should consider opening an employment office and I, sir, am truly not in need of your gratuitous compliments."

Hiram listened somberly. "I am not humoring you my lady. If you find it necessary that I validate my credentials, I assure you that I have viewed the greatest masterpieces in the world."

"Yes, a large portion of the population as visited the Louvre," she cut in.

"Furthermore, not to boast, but my own home displays priceless portraits and landscapes and—"

"I am certain that it does, and frankly I don't have the time to discuss it with you. I am trying to work here."

"I beg your pardon, but I was trying to make a point."

"What point? That you are the world's most renowned art critic?"

"No. I beg your pardon if you have found my advice offensive."

"Is that all you can do is beg my pardon?"

"I was pointing out that I believe myself to be an adequately qualified judge of art and I find this piece to be among the finest. Nothing more, nothing less. If you do not trust my judgment...that is your prerogative," Hiram explained, noticeably irritated and defensive.

Elizabeth sat down in the chair, humbled by the stranger's conviction. A moment later she looked up with questioning eyes.

"In fact, I might suggest that you purchase a potter's wheel, the finest clay and a kiln immediately," Hiram stated with authority.

Elizabeth analyzed the mug which he gently placed in her palms. She stared at it aware that, unfortunately, as fate would have it, although there may be a future in her creation of so many years ago, there were no resources with which to acquire it. Too embarrassed to admit to her financial status, she mumbled, "I'm closing now."

Hiram took one more desperate glance around as the daylight began to drift from the city and the lamplighters came on duty. "I would like to purchase 'Lone Boat'," Hiram offered. Elizabeth shook her head and proceeded to pack up. Hiram watched the woman methodically rewrap each unsold frame in brown paper. Her once glowing face, temporarily lighted with laughter, now appeared glum. He tipped his hat to her upward glance then walked away regretting that his unsolicited advice to the beautiful woman was neither accepted, nor appreciated.

"Good day Elizabeth." Elizabeth gave a slight nod.

On November twenty-seventh Hiram was scheduled to return to Scotland to host the St. Andrew's celebration three days later at McDonnally Manor. However, he found that he could not rid himself of his feelings for the young woman in the square. The Art Exhibit was over and he needed to see her one more time. After a short inquiry with Daniel, he followed his friend's suggestion to visit the local gallery to begin his search for her. The proprietors, Mira and Sean Gillian found Hiram's reference to Elizabeth Clayton as an "artist" to be a bit of an exaggeration. They did, however, supply him with her address after a bit of monetary coaxing.

Hiram left the gallery and went to the quaint teashop, *Berry and Leaves,* to collect his thoughts before venturing to the artist's residence. He removed his hat and entered the shop, lined with shelves offering the customers a variety of jams, conserves, marmalade and several types of tea. He approached the counter, ordered a cup of the house specialty and took a seat at one of the five tables under the windows facing the square. He glanced at the remaining vacant chairs and looked sympathetically to the elderly woman preparing his tea. During a previous visit, she had divulged that the little shop had done very well for itself during the past twenty-four years. However, with the grand opening of the *Crystal Cup*, a teashop extraordinaire with over forty tables and a staff of seventeen, the *Berry and Leaves'* regular clientele began to dwindle. This unfortunate turn of events gave Hiram reason to schedule frequent visits, being a champion of the underdogs of this world.

The frail little woman wiped her hands on her apron, and delivered the hot tea to Hiram's table with a hospitable smile and the same daily greeting, rain or shine.

"Pleasant day, isn't it Hiram?"

Hiram gave his usual response, "Very pleasant indeed, Mrs. Greville." She returned diligently to her post behind the counter to await the possible arrival of the next customer.

Hiram removed his gloves and lifted the cup to his lips when to his astonishment; Elizabeth entered the shop rummaging through her handbag. She paused, extended her hand to the bottom of her bag and pulled out a couple of coins. She smiled with satisfaction and then looked out of the corner of her eye to the customer watching her from the table on her right.

Her smile vanished suddenly with recognition of the gentleman seated three tables away.

Those eyes...isn't it enough that I dream of you every night? In her panic, Elizabeth snapped her bag shut and turned to leave. Hiram rose to his feet and stepped toward her as she reached for the door.

"Please, don't go. Stay and take some tea with me. Please?" he offered her his right arm.

I can't seem to escape you. Why do you have to be so appealing? I feel so inferior.

"Miss Clayton?"

How does he know my name? She looked up to his charming smile and lost all resistance, "Very well," she took his arm and walked to the counter with him. Mrs. Greville nodded and winked at Hiram. Elizabeth scoffed slightly at the two con- spirators.

"Which tea would you desire, Miss Clayton?" he graciously inquired.

"The house tea will be fine."

"My favorite, too," he reached over with his left hand and patted her arm gently which he still held tightly in the crux of his. Naomi looked down at his large hand trying to decide whether or not if she approved of his gesture.

"Would you care for a pastry?"

I would love one, but I am not going to be in- debted to you, any further. "No thank you, sir."

"Mrs. Greville, if you please, she'll have a cou- ple of those biscuits."

"Certainly, Mr. McDonnally."

Do I look that hungry? Maybe you just want to give her the sale.

"Right this way, I am at table three," he led Elizabeth across the room and pulled out the chair across from his.

Isn't he clever? Table three. "This is very kind of you, but what's the occasion?"

"Actually, I was on my way over to your flat, and you have saved me the trip," Hiram explained taking his place across from her.

"And might I inquire as to how you discovered where I live?"

"A simple task, I checked with the gallery."

"And what was your purpose in visiting me, sir?" Elizabeth asked coyly.

Hiram was now at a loss for words. *This woman is so difficult to converse with. She's so hostile. She's not at all like Allison or Naomi.* Hiram shifted slightly. *When up against the wall, turn the tables.*

"Why do you suspect, I was planning to visit you?"

"I'm certain that I haven't the faintest idea as to why," she responded nonchalantly.

Clever woman, yes you do. I've been making a blasted fool of myself ever since I met you.

"Here's your tea and sweets," Mrs. Greville placed the cup and plate of biscuits before Elizabeth and offered a starched linen napkin. "Mr. McDonnally, I want to thank you again for repairing the clock. It keeps perfect time now."

"You are quite welcome, Mrs. Greville." The little woman rushed to the kitchen to remove freshly baked scones from the oven.

"Thank you," Elizabeth called to her while she removed her gloves, placed them in her bag, unfolded the napkin and spread it across her lap. "I would have never imagined you to be a clock repairman," she replied with a hint of sarcasm.

Hiram set down his cup.

"Actually, the McDonnally men, up to this last generation, served in the military. I, on the other hand, became temporarily removed from the McDonnally clan at a young age which presented the opportunity to become an apprentice to a superb clock-smith."

"Opportunity?"

"I took the job out of sheer necessity to eat," he smiled casually.

"You, like the rest of us," she took a sip of her tea followed by another bite of the delicious biscuit.

"Have you always lived in London, Elizabeth?"

"No, I traveled throughout Europe with my parents and sister Eliza."

"Eliza? Eliza and Elizabeth."

"My mother's way of keeping peace in the family. She always did her best to appease everyone."

"I don't understand."

"Eliza is older, three years to the day."

"You were born on the same day?"

"Yes."

"A bit unusual. Did you have a problem sharing your birthday with your sister?"

"Surprisingly, it had its advantages. Traveling like gypsies, our friends were few in number. But when it came time for a birthday party, the combination of hers and mine made for quite a nice group. As to the names, 'Eliza' and 'Elizabeth', it's not that Mama was obsessed with the name, on the contrary, it was hers, Eliza Muriel. She of course wanted to name the first after her. I was supposed to be a son; she was sure of it. She said that only a boy—never mind. I was supposed to be Bernard, after my father. I am certain that he was disappointed to find that the second in line was another daughter. My father insisted that I should be named for his mother."

"Elizabeth," Hiram noted.

"Yes. I think that it has a much nicer ring to it than Eliza. I am also named for my father. My middle name is equally as lovely, 'Bernice.' When I was a child it seemed so special...because it contains the word 'nice.' Sorry, I am rambling."

"You are... *nice,* not rambling."

"Thank you... Do you have any siblings, Mr. McDonnally?"

"Hiram. You may call me Hiram. And yes." Hiram looked away, losing eye contact. "I had a sister."

"I am sorry," Elizabeth blotted her mouth with the napkin.

"No, she may be still living."

"You had a falling out with her?"

"No, I never really knew her. We were separated as infants."

"Oh, I assumed that you lived with both of your parents."

"I did... not really. I lived with my grandmother, my father's mother, and my uncle."

"Your sister stayed with your parents, then?"

"No, my sister Hannah was kidnapped by the nanny."

Elizabeth raised the napkin to her lips and eyes widened. "How horrible for you, Mr. McDonnally. I'm so sorry for you...and all of your family."

"That's quite all right... Please call me Hiram."

"Was she your younger sister?"

"You might say that. You are three years younger than your sister. Mine was three minutes younger."

"A twin, Hiram?"

She says my name with such ease.

"Yes, and I have no idea if she is living or dead. Naturally my family notified Scotland Yard and there was an extensive investigation but, neither she nor the nanny was found."

"Have you tried to search for her?"

"No. I don't remember her, but her presence or should I say 'absence' is something that I live with daily. When do you want to get started with your new business?" he changed the uncomfortable subject.

"I admit, there was some merit to your suggestion. I do enjoy working with clay. I have a nest egg that I was saving, but I planned to purchase a cottage. I have been working for Myrna and Sean for years and only spent enough for painting supplies and the essentials," she explained.

"I know someone who could help you get started. He's a young architect, a friend of the family. He can help you design your studio and your storefront."

"Storefront? I haven't any store."

"I have an idea for that too. I think it would behoove you to meet with him."

"And how do you propose, I do that?"

"At the celebration."

"What celebration?"

"The St. Andrew's celebration... Would you care to join me? I can guarantee that you shan't regret it," he asked nervously.

"And where might that be?

Hiram's smile broadened, "Home."

"Again, where might that be?"

"Lochmoor, of course!"

Elizabeth swallowed the last piece of the biscuit and raised her cup, "Lochmoor it is."

Hiram's heart skipped a beat and tapped his cup to hers, "Capital!"

Chapter VII

"The Return"

Every man according
as he purposeth in his heart,
so let him give;
not grudgingly,
or of necessity:
for God loveth a cheerful giver.

"The master is back! What a beauty," Eloise commented from the parlor window of the McDonnally mansion.

Naomi's eyes rose momentarily, catching sight of her curious friend, "The carriage?" Naomi inquired as she remained seated.

"No, the woman whom he is helping down from the carriage."

Naomi's eyes flashed back up to Eloise, then darted toward the window when her securities red-flagged, as she ran her hand down the side of her face. A trace of jealousy sprung forth from her subconscious with the realization that the man who was once *hers* was sharing company with yet another woman. This was quite a different matter from that of his spending a few innocent months with her daughter in London. A shower of emotion rained down around her as she paused by the sill, watching Hiram lift the bags from the carriage. She then stepped back out of view.

He's not mine, anymore...that's all right, I love Edward. Yes, I love Edward.

"It's true, she's lovely." The handsome couple had turned toward the façade to observe the renovations that Albert had made.

Naomi watched while the green-eyed monster reared its ugly head. *Why does she have to be so appealing?* Hiram and Elizabeth approached the portal. *Why not? Look at him. He's every woman's dream of the perfect—What am I thinking? Who am I to deny him love?*

A surge of energy to counteract her guilt sent her rushing to Eloise's side. "Quick, Eloise! Please prepare some tea and biscuits and use the silver tea set."

"Yes, Mum, but shouldn't I wait to receive them?"

"No, I will. Now, please hurry along!" Naomi scurried to the hall mirror, made a quick check of her hair, reset the silver barrette and put on her best welcoming smile. She ran to the door, tucked her blouse into the waistband of her skirt, took a deep breath and opened the door.

"Hiram, welcome home! Please introduce me to your lovely guest."

"Naomi, may I have the honor of presenting my dear friend, Elizabeth Clayton. Elizabeth this is Naomi McDonnally. Elizabeth will be my house-guest for awhile."

"Hello, Elizabeth."

"My pleasure, Naomi. McDonnally? Are you Hiram's sister? Oh no, that's right, her name was—"

Hiram looked anxiously toward Elizabeth with momentary disapproval. Naomi was stunned that the new friend had crept into Hiram's confidence. *You told her about Hannah? You never talked to me about her.* She put her jealous thoughts in check when Hiram cut in.

"Naomi is married to my uncle, Edward."

Elizabeth cracked a small smile of surprise. Hiram read her thoughts and immediately added, "My very young uncle."

Married to Edward? Although she had been Mrs. Edward McDonnally for decades it sounded strange to Naomi, but found that it had a comforting ring to it, putting her back on track.

"Yes, Hiram has graciously invited us to take up temporary residence here in his beautiful home." Naomi helped them with their coats.

"Oh, you and your husband are visiting?" Elizabeth asked.

Naomi was caught off guard realizing that the curious guest had successfully opened another 'can of worms'.

Hiram sought to explain, "It's a long story. Edward owns the manor we passed, on the other side of the woods, Brachney Hall."

"Oh?" Elizabeth questioned. Naomi led the guests to the parlor to sit.

"How was your journey from London," Naomi struggled to change the subject.

"It was chilly, Mrs. McDonnally, but delightful, thank you," Elizabeth reported.

"*Naomi*, will be fine." *How old does she think I am?*

"The November weather on the moors can be quite refreshing," Hiram interjected.

With Eloise's appearance in the archway, Naomi instructed, "Oh, you may sit that tray right over here. Please have Albert take their bags upstairs, later. Now, please join us."

"Good afternoon Master McDonnally."

"Hello, Louise" Hiram greeted.

"Eloise, sir," the maid respectfully corrected.

"Sorry, Eloise, I haven't had the pleasure of knowing Mrs. Zigmann for very long," Hiram apologized. "But she has been a dear, carrying out my plans for the festivities. Thank you, Eloise."

"My pleasure, sir."

"Oh, did you begin your employ here recently?'" Elizabeth asked.

Hiram and Naomi exchanged nervous glances when Eloise responded proudly, "No Mum, I've been here for years."

Elizabeth turned toward Hiram, who shrugged helplessly. "Elizabeth is a very talented potter!"

"How interesting, Elizabeth," Naomi smiled.

"Hiram, that's very charitable, but—," Elizabeth said timidly.

"Certainly not! I was so impressed with her craft that I am working with her in the construction of her new shop, 'Clayton Creations'. Apropos wouldn't you say? In fact, that is why we are here. Is Guillaume at the manor?" he addressed Eloise.

"No, Sir. He and Allison are visiting with Harriet and the Twiglets," Eloise replied with a renegade grin, anticipating the commotion her comment would perpetuate in mentioning Joseph's carved menagerie.

"I beg your pardon?" Hiram studied the maid's face quizzically.

"Hiram, have some tea and biscuits," Naomi quickly offered.

Once again, rapping at the door sent Eloise scurrying to the central hall. She opened the door for the Master of Brachney Hall, who shed his coat, with her help and gave his hat a toss for the oak rack. The guests viewed the hurling headpiece passing behind the archway. Edward announced, "Bullseye!" and entered the parlor in a full blush as all eyes regarded him.

"Hiram, old man, good to see you!" Edward moved directly to his nephew for a handshake and an embrace, smiling curiously at Hiram's new companion.

"Edward, may I present my guest, Elizabeth Clayton, an expert potter," Hiram smiled proudly. Edward reached for her hand and gently kissed it.

"Well, this certainly is an honor, Miss Clayton," Edward commented, relieved that his nephew was getting on with his life *without* Naomi. He threw an approving glimpse toward Hiram.

"So you are an artist. I, for one, appreciate unique earthenware... not that very few do...appreciate it, that is," Edward stammered, slipping his foot from his mouth. He continued with sincerity, "I would enjoy seeing your work sometime." Now it was Elizabeth's turn to be bombarded with a deluge of unsolicited questions.

"Yes, how long have you been working with clay, Elizabeth?" Naomi asked eagerly.

"Not long," Elizabeth felt a pang of panic inching up her spine.

"Oh, so you have only created a few dozen pieces?" Naomi suggested.

"Actually...one," Elizabeth closed her eyes and confessed nervously.

"Well, even a dozen is quite an accomplishment," Naomi comforted, noting Elizabeth's uneasiness.

"No... only—" Elizabeth began, cut off immediately with Hiram's boost of encouragement.

"Actually, one beautiful mug was the talk of the town; all of London longs for a replica. So, Eloise, when do you expect Guillaume and Allison to return?"

"Shortly, I would imagine, sir. May I pour you some more tea?"

"Yes, please, Eloise."

Muffled laughter in the kitchen grew louder, dissolving the tense parlor exchange. The two little dachshunds sped through the foyer with flopping ears, invisible legs and their heads held high. A skirmish of feet followed close behind. Allison and Guillaume, now quite winded, came to a screeching halt in the archway, trying to catch their breath.

Edward jumped to his feet and joined the two arrivals, "May I present, Hiram's friend, Miss Elizabeth Clayton." Elizabeth nodded and smiled. "Miss Clayton, this is my daughter, Allison O'Connor and Guillaume Zigmann, Eloise and Albert's son."

"My pleasure, Madame." Guillaume walked over and kissed Elizabeth's hand.

My, two in one afternoon, Elizabeth thought.

"This is the young man that I was speaking of, the architect," Hiram explained.

Elizabeth looked to the beautiful Allison, immobile and somewhat disturbed with their meeting. Allison's past also gave rise to her discomfort with Elizabeth. Elizabeth left her chair for a more personal introduction.

"Hello, Allison," Elizabeth spoke softly, "I wasn't aware that you were married," she ascertained by the surname O'Connor.

"I'm not."

Elizabeth hesitated, embarrassed and confused, "I just want to say that I am honored to be here enjoying the afternoon with all of you at Lochness."

"Loch*moor*," everyone corrected in unison. The room lighted with laughter and even Allison's spirits lifted.

Me, married? Mrs. Guillaume Zigmann. Yes, I like that. She reached for Guillaume's hand.

Chapter VIII

"Token of Appreciation"

I have first my master an errand or two.
But I have here from him
a token and a ring;
They shall have most thank
of her that first doth it bring.

—Nicholas Udall

The next morning, Edward busily gathered two shirts and a pair of trousers from his wardrobe. He arranged the mending in a box from the pantry and placed it on the dining room table. He sat down at the writing desk and chose a small piece of parchment and composed a short thank you note addressed to Mrs. Dugan. It read as follows:

I offer my sincere gratitude for consenting to do my mending. You, like all angels, are a lifesaver. Hope this is payment enough for your generosity.

Gratefully, Lucas McClurry

He enclosed a handsome payment for her services. *If she only knew who I really was,* he pondered. It was strange, he felt, still maintaining his Lucas McClurry persona with the village community. He had been successful thus far, in keeping Edward McDonnally lain to rest and out of harms way from Naomi's ruthless father, Nathan. The large framed brute was determined to punish Edward for attacking him the night of Naomi's accident and for terminating his plan to gain control of McDonnally Manor. Lucas McClurry would end the dishonesty and attend his nephew's St. Andrew's celebration as Edward McDonnally.

With thoughts of Naomi, Edward snatched the jacket with the underarm tear from the mending pile. He removed the ring box from its pocket when he heard a cry of pain coming from the grounds behind the mansion. He placed the box on top of Harriet's note and ran towards the cry for help. The aged gardener, Angus had slit his foot in an attempt to saw through a downed branch that blocked the garden path to the tool shed.

"Angus, what have you done?" Edward asked rhetorically.

"Aye, master. What have I done, indeed. Please help me off wi' me boot, sir."

Angus grimaced as Edward gently removed the left boot to reveal the blood-stained woolen stocking. He pulled his white handkerchief quickly from his waistcoat and wrapped it tightly around the injured toes. Edward helped the elderly man to his one good foot and placed a supportive arm around his waist to aid his entry into the mansion. Edward guided Angus to a chair in the kitchen where he found the lacerations to be fortunately superficial. He helped the gardener off with his coat and washed the wounds, then took the first aid basket down from the cupboard and removed the gauze to wrap the wounded foot. His grateful servant apologized for the accident and his poor judgment, while Edward reassured him that Angus was the only one who had suffered a loss. His time and inconvenience were of no consequence.

Naomi's knock at the door sent Edward to greet her. He gave her a quick hug and excused himself to the kitchen with a brief explanation of the accident and his immediate concern for his gardener, who was growing increasingly pale. Naomi followed close behind and agreed that the patient should probably have a sip of water and a cool compress placed on his head after lying down. While Edward carried out the suggestions he asked Naomi to go for Eloise, who had some formal training in nursing, to make a more thorough check of the injured foot.

"Do you want me to take the mending with me now?" Naomi asked.

"Oh, yes, I nearly forgot. That's why you're here. The articles are on the dining room table with a note of thanks and a token payment." He offered the gardener a drink of water, raising his head.

Naomi entered the dining room where she spotted the box of mending with the note sitting beneath the familiar ring box. She dare not touch it, let alone open it. She hesitated then called out to Edward. "What about the little box?" she questioned in disbelief. *This can't possibly be for Mrs. Dugan, can it? There must be some mistake. This is Guillaume's ring for Allison.*

Edward called from the kitchen, "The what?"

Naomi replied with increased volume, her fingers closing tightly around the little box. "The box, does that go with the note?"

"The box? Yes, of course, take the box. Take all of it. Look inside. Do you think it's too much?" Edward asked in reference to the mending articles.

Naomi cracked the ring box; this time with absolute permission. She snapped it shut when Edward repeated the question.

"Naomi! Do you think that it's too much?"

What must you think of me? Carrying on about the ring like that? I thought it was for Allison. Why didn't you say something? Why don't you say something now? Of course, not with Angus present. She then imagined Harriet's joyful expression when she opened the ring box, which faded quickly with the thought of her daughter's disappointment.

"Naomi?" Edward shouted.

"No, no of course not, its fine!" she called, perplexed with the jewel case in her hand. She placed it and the note under the top shirt to keep it from blowing out on her jaunt to the Dugan cottage.

She lifted the mending box, "Goodbye! I'll notify Eloise."

"Thank you, Naomi."

As McDonnally Manor came into view, Naomi saw Harriet leaving to return to her cottage. "Mrs. Dugan! Wait!" Naomi hustled to greet the neighbor and to reluctantly deliver the mending.

"Good morning, Harriet."

"Good mornin' Mrs. McDonnally. How would the wee Heidi be, these days?"

"Well, she has a terrific appetite but hasn't grown much, unlike her playmate Rusty."

"Aye, she was the wee runt of the litter. She willna be much trouble."

"I have Mr. McClurry's mending. He asked me to deliver it to you."

"Strange man, Lucas McClurry. I've yet to meet the man," Harriet noted, peering over Naomi's shoulder at the mysterious Brachney Hall.

"He is quite busy. He takes several business trips a year."

"I wonder," Harriet squinted suspiciously.

"Well, I'm in a bit of a hurry. The gardener at Brachney Hall cut his foot and Mr. McClurry would like Eloise to look at it."

"She'll be comin' out that door, directly. She's fetchin' me a jar of her apple preserves... Aye, here she be."

"Eloise, Angus cut his foot and Mr. McClurry would like you to look at it. Please hurry on over to Brachney Hall."

"Is he hurt badly, Naomi?"

"Not too badly, I believe."

"I should be going then. Here are the preserves, Harriet. Good Day."

"Thank ye, Eloise, Joseph would be thankin" ye too."

"Oh, Mrs. McDonnally, Mr. McDonnally would like to speak with you in the study," Eloise remembered.

"He would? About the celebration?"

"I am not certain. Albert has driven Miss Elizabeth to the village."

"Did Hiram suggest that it was urgent?"

"No, he said to meet with him when you find the time."

"I will, but first I have to speak with Allison. Is she inside?"

"Yes, you'll find her in the parlor with the pups."

"Thank you, Eloise." Naomi handed Mrs. Dugan the box of clothes, considering the possible reasons for the meeting with Hiram. Naomi removed the shirt to reveal the small note and ring box.

Eying the jewel box, Harriet sat the box own on the small stone wall and clipped it from the pile, "Aye, what 'tis this?"

Naomi released a short sigh," There is a note beneath it," Naomi pointed to the folded parchment.

Harriet lifted the note up to her gold rimmed spectacles, opened it and read it silently. "What a dear, dear man! Imagine, pounds and a gift. What e'r could it be?" Harriet slowly lifted the lid of the controversial ring box and immediately raised the back of her other hand to her forehead. "Oh, me darlin' Naomi. I do believe I may faint from the shock."

Naomi quickly offered an arm to the weakened woman. Harriet took a seat on the top of the wall, next to the box of clothing.

"Are you all right, Harriet?"

"I dunna believe I'll be feelin' the same e'r again." The awed recipient of the unexpected gift ran her stout index finger over the glittering jewel. "The stones, they seem to be so real. O' course they canna be authentic. They're green like emeralds. Have ye e'r seen such an incredible ring? I canna believe 'tis mine." Harriet struggled to place the ring on her finger and then flashed it in the sunlight that streamed through a break in the clouds.

I can't believe it either, Naomi pondered, studying the gem that she was certain to be destined for her daughter's hand.

"A wee tight, but the jeweler can fix that. Aye, verra beautiful. What a charmin' man, that Lucas McClurry." Harriet presented her hand with unsurpassed joy for Naomi's inspection. "I'll treasure it for all eternity. Even if it be made o' glass," her eyes twinkled as she admired the gift adorning her chubby finger.

"Yes, he's quite a generous man." Naomi agreed with little enthusiasm, preoccupied with breaking the disappointing news to her daughter.

"What's ailin' ye, Mrs. McDonnally? Now dunna be frettin'. Think o' it! If the Master o' Brachney Hall gives his mendin' lady a ring as beautiful as this, what will he be givin' to his future Mrs.?" Harriet winked with an impish smile. "Good day, Mrs. McDonnally. I need to be gettin' to me mendin'. Dear, dear man..." She shook her head as she headed to her cottage, pausing intermittently to soak up the beauty of the elaborate specimen adorning her hand.

Naomi entered the manor, in deep thought when she found Allison playing on the floor with the puppies in the parlor.

"Allison! What are those puppies doing on the carpet? You know that one accident could destroy it." Naomi reprimanded. Allison scooped up the puppies and gently confronted her mother.

"Mother, what's wrong? You look like you have seen a ghost."

"Worse. I've seen the ring again. Sorry. Brace yourself, Allison. The ring was not intended for you."

"Why do you say that, Mother?" Allison fearfully read Naomi's disappointed face.

"I know because I hand delivered it to Harriet Dugan, only minutes ago."

"Harriet Dugan? It can't be!"

"It's true. She is wearing it as we speak."

"Mother, I just can't believe it." She dropped down in the rocking chair, letting the puppies crawl from her hands to romp playfully on the forbidden rug. "Harriet Dugan? I know Guillaume dotes on his mother... he's always been a mama's boy. But mother, Guillaume with an older woman? I ...well, I wasn't even aware that she and Mr. Dugan were separated." She wrung her hands fretfully.

"Oh, no Allison, of course Harriet and Joseph are still together."

"Has Guillaume lost his mind?"

"No Allison, the ring wasn't from Guillaume."

"I thought you said that Harriet is wearing my engagement ring?"

"It is *not* your engagement ring."

"Not my ring?"

"Actually, it was from Edward."

"Edward? Oh mother, I am so sorry. What is it about that woman? I know that Mrs. Dugan is funny and definitely lovable, but I truly believed that you were the love of his life."

Naomi shook her head and began to laugh, "Allison, he gave it to her as a token of gratitude for doing his mending."

"Mother, *that* ring, as a thank you for *mending*?" Allison cocked her head skeptically.

"Allison, what ever are you implying?"

"Mother, this is the twentieth century."

"Allison, this may be a more liberal age, but we are talking about Edward, a man who was nervous about asking me to look at his stamp collection. Besides, I think the stones are artificial."

"Fakes?"

"Do you believe that Edward would give Mrs. Dugan a ring with real emeralds? Even Harriet knows better."

"I guess you're right..." Allison, disheartened by the misconception, watched the puppies playing tug of war with their knitted doll, when it hit her, "Mother! I'm not getting married! The ring wasn't mine!" Allison rose to her feet.

"Yes, you are. Even though the ring isn't yours, doesn't mean Guillaume isn't going to propose." Naomi offered a comforting hug.

"I suppose you are right."

Guillaume, in search of Rusty, headed down the hall when he overheard the mother and daughter talking. He paused to listen in the shadows.

"I still can't believe Edward gave the ring to Harriet."

"She absolutely adores it."

Guillaume shot straight up from his leaning stance with this news and headed out the back door to Brachney Hall.

"Mother, I have to admit, it was a little more than I would care to wear."

"I'm glad you're not disappointed," Naomi sighed, giving her daughter a quick hug."

"Would you like to take the puppies for a walk, Mummy? I'll fetch the leashes."

"You go ahead; I have to speak with Hiram." Naomi sat down on the sofa reviewing the events of the day, strange as they were. She stared at her wedding band. She had worn it even after the news of Edward's bogus death; but now her dreams of receiving a heartfelt proposal disappeared replaced with nervous thoughts of speaking with her first love.

Guillaume darted through the woods to Brachney Hall with curiosity about the details of the unexpected recipient of the ring. He rapped at the door several times before he opened it and called out to Edward.

"In here, Guillaume," Edward answered with obvious agitation.

In seeing the room in alarming disarray, Guillaume questioned, "Are you looking for something? May I help in the search?" Guillaume offered. "What are we looking for?" he addressed, watching Edward rummage madly through stacks of papers and envelopes of stamps.

"The *ring*, Guillaume, the *ring*!"

"What ring?" Guillaume asked innocently.

"What *ring*! Have you not recovered from that fall yet?"

"The ring that you gave to Mrs. Dugan?"

"What are you talking about?" Edward continued in the hunt.

"I overheard Allison and Naomi discussing the ring that you gave Mrs. Dugan."

"Why would I give Harriet Dugan a ring?"

"I thought that you had decided to dispose of it, since Naomi didn't want it."

Edward stopped to look up at the young man, "Guillaume, what are you jabbering about? Can't you see that I'm in the middle of a crisis?"

"I was standing in the hall and overheard that, Harriet Dugan has a ring from you."

"How would Harriet get my ring...," he stopped and ran his fingers through his hair when the light in his memory flashed like the turning beacon of a lighthouse. "I was helping Angus...the mending...I sat it on top the mending, Guillaume!"

"Sir?"

"I sat the ring box on top of the note, next to the mending when I ran to help Angus this morning. Naomi was kind enough to deliver the mending to Harriet for me, so she wouldn't recognize me as Edward. What must Naomi think?" Edward dropped to a chair. "She thought the ring was for Allison."

"It's perfect, old man... no more problems, no more ring," encouraged Guillaume.

"Guillaume, do you know how much that ring is worth?"

"Oh, right...maybe you should tell Mrs. Dugan that it was a mistake. My father always says lies can tangle you in a web that you may never escape."

"I can't tell her that the ring isn't hers. Naomi and Eloise have told countless stories about Harriet. She may appear to have a heart of stone, but in reality, she is one of the most loved, generous women in all of Scotland. She never asks for anything in return. It would hurt her feelings and she doesn't deserve the disappointment." Once again, Edward chose to forego confrontation and make yet another personal sacrifice.

"That's true. She's my mother's dearest friend...I guess that's it then."

"I guess you're right," Edward sighed. "My only alternative was to sell it at this point, anyway. I wonder what Naomi thinks of all this."

"She didn't seem to be too upset. Want help cleaning up, Sir?"

"No thank you, Guillaume."

"Good day, Sir."

"Good day, Guillaume."

Chapter IX

"Freckleswept"

I've oft been told by learned friars,
That wishing and the crime are one,
And Heaven punishes desires
As much as if the deed were done.

—Thomas Moore

Naomi put thoughts of the ring behind her and faced the doors of the study. This was her first meeting with Hiram since they resolved their differences in October, only a month ago. Although she and Edward were getting along famously, seeing Elizabeth with Hiram induced Naomi's sense of possessiveness of the man she once believed would be her life partner. Her childhood memories with him, his striking appearance, charm and overall appealing character raised havoc in her conscience. For fear of her own feelings, she had avoided moments alone with him. This time she had no alternative but to face her first love and her own demons. She knocked on the pocket door of the study. The door opened and there he stood before her.

"Good Afternoon, Hiram."

"Welcome, welcome, Naomi, thank you for coming," he greeted her with a warm hug, followed by his ever–so appealing smile. "Please, have a seat. May I offer you some refreshment, some tea, perhaps?"

No sooner was she in the room before she found herself admiring his perfect construction, the well-groomed beard and inviting smile— the same smile of eighteen years ago.

"No thank you, Hiram." *How could I eat anything right now?* "Actually, I haven't been eating much of late."

"Oh? Have you been ill?" he asked with concern.

"No, I have been preoccupied with a number of issues." She made little effort to hide her disappointment.

"Yes?"

"Now, enough about me, I need to be honest with you...I was a bit taken a back when I learned that you had confided in...Elizabeth about Hannah's abduction," she said in a mildly accusing tone.

"Naomi, it was purely serendipitous on her part. She asked if I had any siblings. I felt that there was no harm in telling her the truth; it *is* common knowledge."

"Of course, Hiram. I meant that I was surprised that you had never shared your sister's disappearance with me," Naomi said pointedly. *That is not what I wanted to say. All right, I don't care that you know that I'm jealous.*

"Naomi?" This defensive response was not at all what he expected. Naomi looked away indignantly.

"Sorry if you took offense, but I have asked you here today for that very purpose. When Elizabeth mentioned Hannah, I noticed your discomfort. I have been wrestling with the guilt of dismissing the entire abduction incident and I preferred to consult with someone more familiar. When I met you, we were little more than children. I wanted only your love, not your pity. It was enough that I burdened you with my ill-feelings for my father. I chose to leave my mother's infirmary and all the other sordid details buried in the past. I didn't know if you had heard about my twin or not. I have been trying to renew my life. Elizabeth is a wonderful woman, but I have met with her only recently and I am not comfortable discussing my past with her." Naomi regained eye contact.

Isn't that exactly how you felt about me?

"With you, Naomi there *are* no secrets." She was humbled by the vote of confidence.

Naomi wasn't prepared for this comment and her guilt was no longer idle, leaving her no other choice but to confess. He was too attentive, too sincere and genuine to deceive.

"I'm flattered Hiram. That is not altogether true. I have something that I need to tell you. You may, quite possibly, lose all respect for me."

"Lose respect for you? I can't imagine, Naomi. What are you referring to?"

"Hannah. I have known about her for several weeks," she admitted fearful that this first intimate conversation would come to a screaming halt.

"Edward, of course. He informed you."

"No, I like Elizabeth, found out purely by accident...I suppose 'purely' is a poor choice of word. Hiram, I was in your mother's bedroom."

"On the third floor?" Hiram moved in closer, withholding a smile, being familiar with Naomi's inquisitive nature.

"Yes, I never meant to trespass, but the key was in the door and I admit that I gave into my impulsiveness."

"That doesn't explain how you discovered the information about my sister."

"I read about her abduction in the letter from your father," she continued, knowing he would soon lose any admiration for her.

"A letter?"

"I came across a little trunk, under the bed..."

"Nomee..." Hiram reprimanded gently, "under the bed?"

"I wasn't *ransacking* the room. Patience was under the bed and wouldn't come out, when she did, she knocked the case from my hands."

"Patience?"

"My cat."

Naomi's head dropped and she said nothing. Hiram sat next to her, waiting for her to continue when he noticed her shoulders starting to quiver and her hands moved quickly to wipe the tears streaming down her cheeks. She cried for the loss of her pet, but she was equally crying for the loss of this loving man.

"Oh, Nomee," he comforted her gently as closed his arm around her.

"I loved that cat," she sobbed. "I didn't know that her time had come...I knew she wasn't feeling well. I would have gone to look for her...I...I thought she wanted..." she broke down and cried for several minutes in his arms. She felt so safe and protected there.

Hiram's heart went out to her, finding that Naomi was still the tenderhearted girl from his youth. "Nomee, it was her time. She probably needed to go off alone. She couldn't bear to see you upset. God knows it was best for both of you. You gave her a wonderful life. Come on now, cheer up, love," Hiram gently coaxed. "Would you like some tea?"

"Yes, please," she sniffled as she withdrew her handkerchief and wiped away the remaining tears. *You are so caring. You haven't changed. I need you.*

Hiram left the study and returned with the refreshment and a couple of Eloise's biscuits.

"I thought these might help," he offered the treats scattered on the tray. She felt the warming comfort of his returning presence.

"Thank you." Naomi folded her hankie and placed it in her pocket and sipped the tea while Hiram took his place beside her. "Would you care to go on with your ...your story?" he asked tenderly.

"Yes. I didn't open the case. Patience knocked it out of my hands. It contained the letter and some infant articles. I read the letter. I hope that you know that I never meant to disrespect your parents' privacy, Hiram."

"What was the exact content of the letter?"

"Not too much." Naomi hesitated, unsure of Hiram's response when she mentioned his father's intentions. "Your father...your father was involved in a search for your nanny, Vila, along with the investigation in Europe, with no results."

Hiram listened intently to Naomi's summary. "Is that all?" he questioned with indifference.

"No."

"Go on."

"Your father apologized to your mother for his absence while he was stationed in Africa. He promised to love her and keep you safe. He said that he would pray for your sister's safety."

The unresolved feelings for his father led Hiram to leave the sofa and retreat to the fireplace. He stood silently absorbed in the flickering flames, his hands clasped behind his back.

Naomi sat, watching and waiting nervously, knowing Hiram's explosive nature. *How well I know you, Hiram. Your pain runs deep. It always has. My poor dear man... your heart is made of glass. It's been shattered so many times. Will your contempt for your father continue to haunt you?*

Hiram watched the last twig split and fall between the slots of the grate to sizzle in the embers. The tears never came, the anger toward his father and animosity for the nanny was suppressed and compressed to remain latent in his subconscious. The emotion was there, but remained in check by his newfound happiness.

A minute later he turned slowly back to Naomi, smiled sincerely and took his place beside her. He looked off into space then took her right hand in his, and looked deep into her green sympathetic eyes.

"Nomee, do you think that I should try to find her?"

"If you feel the need, I think we should try."

"We?"

"I will help all that I can, Hiram. I *have* had a bit of experience with mysteries. The search may be difficult, but most worthwhile endeavors are. I think we should be optimistic, but realistic. We may not find her."

"Yes, one seldom knows where the road will lead, does one?" he added with an air of despondency.

"Yes, the unknowns *are* intimidating."

"All right," he squeezed her hand and with a wink and a positive attitude announced, "We'll start in a week or two, if that will not interfere with your plans. I will be leaving to London with Elizabeth on the first. I'll be returning the following week."

"That will be perfect. Edward is leaving for Leederveen, that week on business."

With this unexpected remark, Hiram verified with concern, "I never intended for this search to be concealed from Edward," he quirked a brow.

"No, no. I meant that it will leave time for the two of us to devise a plan because Edward is preoccupied with business of his own. I have to tie up some loose ends with the Burn's Night preparation, but other than that I am free to assist you...You will be attending Burns' Night at Brachney Hall, won't you?"

"May I bring a guest?"

"Elizabeth?" she asked in disbelief. *Are you not feeling what I feel?*

"If you wouldn't mind," Hiram waited skeptically for her answer.

"I have a limited guest list," she said with some degree of panic. Seeing his curious disapproval, quickly amended, "Yes, naturally. I would be delighted for Elizabeth to attend." She forced a confused smile.

"Capital, we'll be there, and can I be assured that we'll be enjoying your company for St. Andrew's Day?"

"Of course." Naomi sat her teacup on the table and stood. He rose from his place on the sofa.

"Very well. Is there anything else you care to discuss?" He looked down at her with a gentle gaze that cut through to her jealous heart.

Why did you mention her? Yes, I have something more to discuss. Why her? Why Elizabeth? her inner voice called out.

"Naomi?"

Startled, Naomi quickly responded, "I'm sorry, my mind was wandering. Nothing more, I guess we are finished for today."

"Are you certain?" he asked detecting her disturbed tone.

With this last opportunity, Naomi was ready to disregard all respect for herself and the consequences and throw herself at him. But then, he spoke.

"I will talk with you later, Nomee," his dark eyes danced with hope and contentment.

Naomi paused, then turned to him questioning, *Why do you still call me 'Nomee' if you don't care?* She was ready to confess that the old feelings for him had returned when he placed his large protective arm over her delicate shoulders. His mere touch sent a rushing sensation that momentarily stole her breath away. He led her to the door.

When they reached the hall, Hiram took Naomi's hands in his while she silently prayed for those special words to cross his lips.

He looked gratefully down at her, "I never believed I would have such a wonderful aunt. Please give Edward my best wishes for a safe journey."

Naomi stood numbed by shock and disappointment. She gave a quick nod and walked toward the kitchen. Once out of view, she ran to the cot in the adjoining maid's room. She threw herself down on the mattress, burying her sobs in the pillow. After a minute she turned over facing the ceiling, flushed with tears of remorse. She folded her hands so tightly that her knuckles were turning white as she begged for forgiveness.

"Dear Lord, what have I been doing? What's the matter with me? Forgive me, please forgive me, I do love Edward...not Hiram," she cried, her eyes closed. A familiar feminine voice resounded through her sobs.

"I will tell you what's the matter with you, Mum."

Naomi raised her face in shame, "Oh Eloise," she shook her head in disbelief of her deplorable behavior. "I didn't know you were here. How is Angus?"

"Mum, he's fine and you are too. Listen to me. You may continue with your prayers; I will not interrupt. Or you may take a minute to listen to an old woman with a little experience in this area," Eloise offered with an understanding smile. "Don't be embarrassed. You were swept back in time for a bit —you were once very much in love with Hiram and his charisma, not to mention, his deep penetrating irresistible eyes and that gorgeous head of curls. Oh, yes, we all take notice. I may be an old woman but if my Albert looked... never mind."

Naomi bit her bottom lip to restrain the determined straggling sobs, unsure of the direction her friend was headed with the unexpected comments. Naomi sat up and motioned for Eloise to sit beside her. Eloise placed a loving arm around her and continued sympathetically.

"Mum, I know that you and Master Hiram shared something wonderful when you were younger. Remember, I was there in the parlor to clean up the aftermath of that failed relationship. He was your heart and soul, back then. The present conveniently slipped into hiding while you found yourself alone with him with all his charm and the closeness of the past relationship."

"How did you know?"

"I was at the top of the stairs after you finished your meeting with him. I saw the look on your face."

"But I am with Edward, now?"

"Of course you are and you love him dearly. You were just freckleswept. It happens everyday to people everywhere," Eloise explained with expertise.

"I beg your pardon? Freckleswept?" Naomi asked, blotting her eyes with the hankie from her skirt pocket.

"Well, that's what I call it. With you, maybe it's 'curlswept'. It occurs when a cherished trait of a loved one from our past triggers a cart load of feelings. You know, eyes, smile, dimples; with me it was freckles, Daniel's freckles."

"Daniel?" Naomi asked suspiciously.

"Yes, Daniel. It doesn't really matter which Daniel. Mr. Zigmann nor anyone else, needs to be frettin' over Daniel," Eloise added defensively.

"Oh, Eloise, I never meant," Naomi was cut off as Eloise continued with her left index finger tapping at her temple searching her brain for the details.

"Well, let's see...yes, I was about your age. Albert and I had recently relocated to Paris with Guillaume. He was only two or three, at the time...cute little guy. Still is don't you think?"

"Guillaume or Albert?" Naomi mocked behind her hankie. Eloise gave Naomi an *aren't you clever* look.

"Now don't distract me while I'm remembering that handsome Daniel," she smiled like a girl in her teens." Actually, I was at the train station waiting for my sister Lillian to arrive when I found myself standing smack beside Daniel. Well, I was in a

state of temporary shock, I was! You can imagine."
Naomi gave an affirmative with a nod.

"Why, I hadn't laid eyes on Daniel since I was twenty-one in Frankfort. Oh...I was so young and impetuous back then. Daniel worked at the bookstore. I remember that first moment when I saw him, just like it was yesterday. I excused myself...he was busy unwrapping a new shipment, when I asked if he had a copy of Shakespeare's plays."

"Why Eloise, I had no idea that you were—"

"I wasn't. I had never read Shakespeare and had never any inclination to read it. It popped into my head for lack of any other impressive title. You see, his copper hair intrigued me."

"Oh..." Naomi pictured a younger Eloise proudly making the request.

"I'll tell you Mum, when that young man turned around; I nearly died and saw the Golden Gates flash before me. There he stood. The brightest freckled faced young Irishman, you'd ever imagine. Needless to say, it was love at first sight; I fell head over heels in record time. Then he was gone, like a flash in the night, off to Ireland."

"Did you exchange letters?"

"No, we had decided that there was no point in corresponding. It was highly unlikely that our paths would cross again. But you see, like you and Master Hiram, our relationship didn't end properly; left hanging there, like laundry in the rain. When I saw him in the station, he turned and there they were, those adorable freckles, still sprinkled across his cheeks, right over the bridge of his nose." Eloise paused, mesmerized by the vision of Daniel's dappled face.

"Of course he had matured, Naomi, we all had, but for a moment I was freckleswept back to the bookstore, that winter long ago in Germany. We started reminiscing after we had nearly squeezed the stuffing out of one another. The next thing I knew, I was having coffee with him at a small shop down the street."

"What about Lillian?" Naomi curiously interjected.

"Yes. What about Lillian?" Eloise slowly shook her head with disapproval. "My poor sister waited at the station for nearly two hours while I was freckleswept abroad over four cups of coffee and three pieces of stolen. I never heard the end of it and was as guilt ridden as the day when I was but four years old and had unrolled nearly every ball of my mother's yarn. I guess that's why your Patience, God bless her, always aggravated me when she dove into my knitting basket. Guilty memories, I guess." Naomi smiled, this time, with yet another memory of her beloved cat.

"You see, Naomi, you're only human; freckleswept, curlswept, it doesn't matter. You know honestly where your loyalty and love lies. Why like you, I bawled like an infant when I got home from the station. The moment my eyes met my adoring Albert and saw my sweet baby Guillaume playing on the blanket, I felt like a faithless hussy, even though it was an innocent meeting of sorts."

Eloise's testimony began to successfully smooth the wrinkles in Naomi's conscience. The insightful housekeeper's explanation seemed to make perfect sense.

"Lillian had eventually found her way to our flat and of course she thought that my breakdown was all out of contrition for abandoning her...Now, I want you to do something, Naomi," Eloise advised motherly.

"All right, Eloise."

"Close your eyes and go back to the evening when you and Edward came to our cottage; the evening Edward first met Guillaume."

Naomi complied and recounted, "Yes, I remember. That was the day that you took Guillaume to Gavonshire to see Doctor Kelly after his accident."

"Yes...you and I moved to the kitchen table to chat and I was carrying on about the doctor."

"Yes, you were very impressed with him. Did he have freckles too?" Naomi teased.

"No, Mum, but he blessed me with a good health report for my son. Now close those green eyes...Do you remember what you were all fired up about?"

Naomi smiled peacefully. "Yes, the perfect picnic with Edward."

"Remember the story you told me about that the stew and the ducks?"

"Yes, I'll never forget...we were first getting to know each other. Edward and I were drawn together, so naturally...but at the same time we were nervous and awkward, like young people courting. And then, Duncan Ridge. Yes, Duncan Ridge," her smile broadened as her heart swelled with love for Edward and the driving force he had become in her life. Naomi opened her eyes, content with her life back in focus.

"Thank you, Eloise, you are a dear friend, as always," she reached for an appreciative hug.

"Eloise, it shan't happen again, will it? You know, being freckleswept?" Naomi asked with concern.

"There are no guarantees. It may tug at your ear a little, but you will not lose your way again."

"How do you know?"

"Because, I've seen it happen, time and time again. One thing I've found: if one is freckleswept and is sincerely contrite the first time, one is left with a bookmark in their memory on the page titled, 'Never Again.' However, if one treats their interest and the possible repercussions with little consequence-beware! History will repeat itself over and over until they have destroyed the relationship with their current partner. Take Ruth, for example."

"Ruth from the Bible?"

"No, no Ruth from Heathercrest. She was shyswept."

"Shyswept?"

"Yes, shyswept. She met this man who owned the sweet shoppe. Everyone knew who he was but, no one really knew him. Do you know what I mean? Let's see, what was his name?"

"Yes, like Ben at Stanton Manor."

"Exactly. Ruth, liked to mother shy men, having never been a mother herself. She was married to a miner, who seemed to have little time for her. They rarely left their home together. Ruth started visiting the sweet shoppe regularly. Besides putting on a few pounds, well, next thing we knew, she was leaving her husband. I met her once at the shop on a day both her and her new husband were working. What a sorry sight, he was reprimanding her every two seconds, 'fill the trays and roll more bonbons'. Then, 'clean the chocolate vats and sweep up that mess.' You couldn't help but feel embarrassed and a bit sorry for poor Ruth. She had led a life of leisure with the miner; he didn't care if she ever lifted a finger for housekeeping. Now she's married to a shoppe, that is anything but sweet. Twelve hours a day, no less."

"I guess that goes with 'be careful what you wish for,'" Naomi added seriously.

"Don't you worry, Mum. Master Hiram may light a spark in your heart, but Edward will give you fireworks that will forever light your spirit."

"That's beautiful, Eloise. Is that how you feel about Albert?"

"Mum, when Albert and I attend a social gathering and say we've been talking in our various circles of friends, not paying any attention to one another; it never fails, one of us will glance over at the other and the second our eyes meet, we become deaf to all voices in the room. We seem to be standing alone in the crowd, reading each others thoughts, sharing a bond that can withstand the test of time. It's very simple knowing that you belong together, but it's difficult to stay together at times. Mum, you love mysteries and puzzles. Did you ever put a jigsaw puzzle together?"

"Of course, as a child, many times."

"Did you ever try to move the completed one from one table to another?"

"Yes, it's impossible without the aid of a board or tray of some kind to put beneath it for support."

"That's the way I believe relationships are. In the beginning you try to keep your relationship in perfect order but, once you start moving through time, without a strong base, bit by bit, piece by piece, the perfect picture is destroyed and lost."

"And the base, Eloise?"

"Your faith in each other, in the relationship and in God. He will steer you in the right direction."

"Eloise, I haven't given Edward the appreciation that he deserves. Do you know that he calls me? His magic square."

"His what?"

"Magic square. He was so incredibly sweet. He drew a picture in the dust of a square, a square in which all the numbers add up to be the same sum." Seeing Eloise's perplexed expression, Naomi tried to clarify the significance to Edward's strange behavior.

"It was an illustration of his love for me. He says that I am his magic square, perfect from every angle. I'm not, but he still loves me. Isn't he absolutely wonderful?"

"A little strange, but wonderful, indeed. Now, dear, you will be fine. You do seem a bit edgy of late."

"I know. I am tired, very tired, emotional stress, I guess. I have so many errands to run before the Burn's Night party. I have tried to keep the guest list manageable. I have invited the Kilverts, the Dugans, the Wheatons, and of course Hiram."

"And Elizabeth," Eloise added tactfully.

"Yes, and Elizabeth."

"Oh, Mum I'll help you all that I can, but why don't you curl up in that comfortable chair in the parlor. I'll stoke the fire. Master Hiram as left for the day."

"Sounds tempting, Eloise."

"You know you want to look refreshed when the fireworks arrive! Then off you we go!" Eloise offered an arm and the two parleyed down the hall with Heidi following playfully at their feet. Naomi situated herself in the chair while Eloise pulled the ottoman beneath her feet, pulled the quilted coverlet from the woven wicker chest and then tucked it around her exhausted friend. "Sleep well. I'll wake you at tea time." Eloise smiled down at her dear friend hoping the master of Brachney Hall would soon propose and give sweet Naomi the *ring*.

"Thank you, Eloise." Naomi closed her eyes, then reopened them, when she heard a tiny whimper. A tiny head appeared over her feet. Heidi sat patiently on her haunches, upright and waving her paws frantically in perfect dachsie form.

"Oh, Heidi, you've mastered it! Aren't you a talented little lassie. That deserves a boost! C'mon little one, up you go" Naomi bent over and lifted the pleased pup to her favorite spot, Naomi's lap. Heidi snuggled into the coverlet and with one last blink at her proud owner, closed her tiny dark eyes and fell to dream of days frolicking with Rusty. Heidi, like Naomi, was having difficulty filling the void that came with the passing of Naomi's beloved cat, Patience, Heidi's surrogate mother. However, Patience's lessons were well-remembered. Heidi would sit perfectly still on the window seat, watching the birds, only a pane away. Likewise, the puppy had mastered the skill of balancing on the upper edge of the over-stuffed chair back and had earned her feline mother's title as Eloise's Favorite Mischief-maker, hiding her yarn balls or climbing into the housekeeper's basket of clean laundry.

It was not uncommon on days when Naomi felt sure that Heidi had recovered from her loss that she would find her little friend curled up in Patience's lonely basket. Heidi's tiny round chimpanzee-like eyes exhibited a haunting intelligence with thoughts and no words to express them. Naomi would gently lift the little dog from her memories and hug her close with a promise to enjoy this little character every day, truly believing that a pet is a gift that adds love and laughter to that chapter of one's life.

At the Dugan cottage, Joseph had returned from the fields to wash and prepare for his noon meal, when he found his wife seated at the kitchen table polishing her new acquisition with a scrap of white silk and an admiring smile.

"What ye be polishin' there, Love?"

"Just a wee token of appreciation from the Master of Brachney Hall for mendin," she announced holding up the ring for her husband to get a better view.

He bent down as his eyes poured over the jewels, "Let me have a look see... Gaudy as all get out. "

"Bite ye tongue, Joseph Dugan. Ye should be the first to recognize a piece o' art!" Harriet turned the ring over several times in her opened palm. In an instant, the curious spouse snatched the jewel and held it up to the lighted window.

"Joseph, ye hands are filthy, have ye been crawlin' through the fields like a babe?"

"Ne'r ye mind me hands, they be puttin' food on the table. These are workin' hands," he added as he inspected the gift. Harriet grabbed the ring and began polishing it fervently.

"Look what ye done. 'Tis a mess now! Joseph, 'tis a wee tight on me wee fingers and I would be needin' the cart to take it to Mr. McDenby to fix it."

"Mr. McDenby, eh? I seen the man lookin' at ye like a fresh catch o' herrin'! Ye'll be stayin' right here. I'll be takin' it to town and ye willna say another word about it," Joseph concluded as he filled the basin with water to wash his hands and face.

"Don't be losin' it Mr. Dugan! I've no shown it to me dear friend, Eloise yet!"

"Have ye no ears, woman. I said nay another word!" Joseph took his place at the little table while his silenced wife served the meal in a huff.

The next morning, Joseph placed the ring box in his satchel with the round of cheese that he retrieved from the pantry and headed to the village.

Once at the quaint jeweler's office, he presented the ring to Mr. McDenby. The jeweler opened the box without hesitation.

"'Twas a gift for Mrs. Dugan and it need be larger," Joseph explained.

"Aye, what an elegant specimen. Yer a frugal man, Joseph Dugan, but ye musta saved ye whole life for this one!"

"I ne'er purchased it! A customer o' Harriet gave it to her for mendin'," Joseph disclaimed adamantly.

"Aye? Who would be the wealthy one, if ye dunna mind me inquirin'?"

"The ring, it be valuable?"

"Aye, in all me years in the business, ne'r I had the pleasure of holdin' a beauty as elegant as this in me verra own hands," the jeweler stared with awe at the gem. Aye, Mr. Craig's handiwork; the jeweler eyed the label in the box lid.

"Dunna be foolin' wi' me Mr. McDenby," Joseph warned.

"I be tellin' the gospel truth – it's worth a fortune!"

"Tell me Joseph, who would be so indebted to bestow such a treasure on your missus?"

"Ne'r ye mind," the irate husband snatched the box, closed it and deposited it in his satchel.

"Good-day Mr. McDenby," Joseph offered as he headed toward the door.

"Do ye not want it sized, Mr. Dugan?" the surprised storekeeper called out, cut short by the slamming door. "Aye, what a beauty...who would be so generous?" he pondered, tapping his fingers on the desk.

Joseph ripped a hunk from the round of cheese, stuffed it in his mouth and urged Jock homeward.

The spirits of your fathers
Shall start from every wave,
For the deck it was their field of fame,
And ocean was their grave.

—Thomas Campbell

Chapter X

"Tavy"

But now it has fallen from me,
It is buried at sea;
And only the sorrow of others
Throws its shadow over me.

—Henry Wadsworth Longfellow

Harriet sat rigid in the armless rocker, aggressively winding and whipping the yarn from the wooden needles creating the sleeve of the dark woolen sweater for her husband, Joseph. He had remained a sailor at heart and refused to let his dry-docked life convert his fashion sense that was based purely on utility. Thus, his daily wardrobe consisted of the knitted ganser and mud pants with the typical leather straps buckled beneath his knees to protect his trouser cuffs from the reappearing puddles.

His wife had joined Mrs. Kilvert and her daughter, Helen, for the annual journey to Duncan Ridge to scrape lichen for the dye. These buckets of gathered crotal were then cooked with the layered wool to produce the deep rich hue. The wool, that now slipped rapidly through Harriet's fingers, was a labor of love, a product of hours of preparation whereas, Mrs. Kilvert's would find it's way to the village mercantile in the form of fine tweed fabric.

Harriet made one last purl stitch, and bound off the row with her usual speed. She mumbled to herself, grumbling over her husband's short temper and inability to see reason, then lay the sweater in her lap. Harriet removed her specs and rubbed her eyes.

"Aye Joseph, ye be makin' me angry beyond words. How can a man, a lovin' husband who spent his savin's for that spinnie, a beauty o' a spinnin' wheel, turn tail and run to that horrid butcher Jon Wiggins? Believin' me to be carryin' on wi' that wealthy Lucas McClurry," she shook her head in frustration.

She eyed the delicate spinning wheel sitting next to the fireplace. "It was a bonny day when I gave me ol' muckle wheel to Maryanne and set me fine spinnie in the parlor," she sighed in the memory, then returned to thoughts of her belligerent husband. She scowled and folded the sleeve of the sweater inside the front, rolled it up, and dropped it carelessly into the large knitting basket next to the chair.

A rap at the door signaled her dachshund, Angel, to her post on the gray upholstered footstool by the front window. A series of sharp barks alerted that the visitor was a stranger. Harriet peeked cautiously out the portal window of the door, when she was met by the brown eyes of a young man she thought to be about Guillaume Zigmann's age. She opened the door and asked bluntly, "Weel, what would ye be wantin' laddie?"

"Would this be the home o' Joseph Dugan?"

"Aye...and who would be askin'?" Harriet scowled, further perturbed with her husband's absence.

"Henry McTavish, they call me Tavy. I have somethin' for Mr. Dugan, somethin' from me father, Patrick McTavish."

"Come on in out o' the cold. And what would that somethin' be?"

"Thank ye. This is me father's leather coat. He was lost in the last storm in his dingy, the Bonnie Ellen, named for me mother. This note was in his strong box." He handed the folded paper to Mrs. Dugan, and she read it aloud.

I LEAVE ME LEATHER COAT TO JOSEPH DUGAN, THE ONLY MAN ON THIS EARTH WITH STRENGTH ENOUGH TO BEAT ME ARM WRESTLING. PATRICK MCTAVISH

"Aye...me husband has many a tale o' how he tried to get yer father to bet the coat, but he ne'r would." She ran her hand over the tanned leather garment with brass buttons. "Joseph will wear it proudly. Sorry, laddie, must ha' been terrible for ye."

"Aye, I miss me father, but I have me crew. Father was the last o' me livin' relatives."

"Well, Henry we'd be delighted to have ye stay for a bit, Joseph should be returnin' soon for his supper. Come on in the kitchen and take some tea wi' me."

"Thank ye, Mrs. Dugan. Ye'r verra kind." He pulled his woolen cap from his head and passed through the parlor in the usual state of awe, as he admired the dioramic shelving featuring the "Twig-lets", Joseph's hand carved creations.

The little dachshund found the guest to be quite agreeable and stayed close at his heels.

"Would this be a museum?"

"No, me husband's handiwork."

"Aye, the 'Twiglets', I spied the shingle o'er the door. I have one o' me own." He reached into his pocket and pulled out a carved wooden whale about three inches long, and presented it to his hostess. "This one belonged to me father."

Harriet smiled with recognition of her hus-bands art work, and pointed to the mammal's dou-ble, beached on the fourth shelf. "Fashioned the backdrops meself."

"Ye'r pullin' me leg, they look like me picture postcards."

"Ye have friends ye be correspondin' wi'?"

"No, I collect the cards. I be lackin' in any talent o' me own."

"I don't believe it. The Lord blessed all us wi' talent o' some sort. Fishin' may be yer talent. Come sit wi' me in the kitchen and warm yerself by the stove. Ye have a lassie ye'r partial to Henry?" Harriet asked keenly, as she poured a cup of tea for her guest. Henry turned three shades of pink before answering.

"No, Mrs. Dugan," he replied as he took a seat at the table.

"Ye'r quite the handsome lad. Ye need to spend more time in the ports and less out at sea. Me Joseph was gone for months at a time; I barely had a chance to hook him afore he was off and runnin' again. I mended for him, made a few coats too. Aye, Joseph was an eye catcher back then."

She stopped stirring the stew, stared off into space momentarily, then wrinkled her nose in disgust at her husband's current attitude. She continued with the meal preparation, lifting a large bowl of vegetables from the table and pouring them into the pot of boiling water while Tavy spoke of his family.

"Me parents met in Shetland. Mother was a fish gutter. Me father carried a picture o' Mother wearin' her apron wi' her fingers bandaged. When I was a wee one, I asked Father if she be a poor fish gutter. He laughed and said that they be protection for her delicate fingers and she was one of the fastest gutters in all Britain, fifty fish a minute. Aye, her picture was next to his heart when he met his maker. When she stopped followin' the fleets, she spent ten hours a day baitin' hooks. Father said she'd bait nye onto fifteen-hundred hooks."

"Aye, three mussels to a hook, ye separate the lines in sculls, baskets lined with grass, to keep'em from tanglin'," Harriet added with a professional tone. "I baited a few lines meself, one summer wi' me cousin, Mary."

"Aye?"

"It be hard work I tell ye. Gave it up to open me mendin' shop. We would bait while my uncle was reddin' the lines, at Aberdeen. We would go down to the quay o' Campbeltown pier and watch the herrin' come in, about seven-hundred-and fifty to a cran basket. A sight to behold! The port would be lined wi' the white-striped bows o' the Fifies and the gutters and the packers would be gleamin' with fish scales. Went out wi' Mary and me uncle Sam once wi' the ring nets. We were in the dingy that circled 'round the herrin' school. Have much schoolin' Henry?"

"Some. Me mother was killed on the docks; rest her soul. Two brawlin' drunkards were fightin' or' a woman when one pulled a knife... her face ..." Tavy paused and looked sadly down at the tea cup. "She was in the wrong place at the wrong time. Me father says... *said* that she's an angel in heaven, baitin' the hooks that snag the hearts o' young ones; a cupid o' sorts. He said she had more love in one o' her beautiful eyelashes than most people have in their entire body. She's waitin' to bait mine. Doesna think I be ready yet, I suppose."

Harriet wiped her eyes with her apron. "Steams gettin' in me eyes." Harriet turned back to her pot. "Yer mother would be proud o' ye, Henry McTavish. Any more to yer brood?"

"No sisters o' brothers." Spotting the basket by the rocker in the parlor, he remarked, "I see ye knit, too."

"Makin' a ganser for Mr. Dugan, He ne'r really left the sea."

"Father said when a man gets saltwater in his veins, the sea is in him for eternity. Me mother knitted. I have her leather knittin' belt and her needles; all I have o' me mother's."

"Aye the gutters were flittin' 'bout the quay wi' balls o' yarn pinned to their aprons, waitin' for the fish." Harriet stirred the stew with the long wooden spoon. "More tea, laddie?"

"No, thank ye." Tavy leaned back in his chair. "I worked ashore for a time. Father's sayin' was 'if there be any doubt, take time out. Ye have to keep yer mind on yer work ev'ry second at sea or ye be endangerin' yeself and ye mates.' I worked at Finzean saw mill on the Water o' Feugh."

"Aye, in the forest o' Birse at Aberdeenshire," Harriet commented after she sipped the stew.

"Didna last long, the water reminded me o' the sea and was back board ship in six months."

Harriet took another taste of the stew, "Needs salt. Joseph loves a good plate o' herrin', pickled and smoked in the kiln. I dinna ken what's keepin' him. Ye be lookin' like ye be needin' some shut eye, Henry."

"I'm fine, thank ye." He reached down and petted the little dog at his feet.

"Ye take a wee nap afore supper. Ye can sleep in the cot in the back room."

"Would ye be certain it willna be a problem, Mrs. Dugan?"

"Get yer self goin' laddie, I'll be callin' ye when supper's ready. I have yet to fix the baps. "

"I'm obligin' to ye, Mrs. Dugan." The sleepy-eyed guest took her advice and laid his father's coat on a crate next to the door of the backroom and stretched out on the cot while Harriet prepared the Scottish bread.

With the loss of the company of the new found friend, Angel retired to her basket, now absent of her litter. The little dachsie rolled over and lay on its back with all fours extending upward.

"Aye, ye'r provin' Joseph right, you must be in trainin', Angel." Joseph was convinced that the pup would soon be ready to take the bottom pyramid position in the the Barnum and Bailey Circus. The little dog was no sooner settled in with head back and tip of its tongue sticking from its muzzle, when the creaking of the shed door sent the little dog into a sprint toward the backdoor of the cottage. The favorite lap had returned.

Joseph unhitched the mule, removed the harness and turned out the reluctant animal, preferring a few flakes of hay in the confines of the shed, to the pasture. Nevertheless, after a squeal followed by a few disapproving kicks targeted at the fence and Joseph's reprimand, the mule was left to wait for its evening meal. Joseph entered the cottage and greeted Angel, then tossed the ring case on the kitchen table.

"Here's ye crown jewels, Harriet!"

"Keep yer voice down, Joseph Dugan."

"Ye think that 'cause ye have a ring worth more than me entire estate that I'll be yer whimperin' lacky?"

"What ye be sayin', Joseph?" Harriet asked with alarm.

"Yer wee token of appreciation is worth a fortune!"

"It must be a mistake," Harriet dropped to the wooden chair and examined the jewel.

"No mistake, Harriet! Ye will be returnin' it now and be rid o' the man o' I will!"

In a defensive whisper Harriet demanded, "Joseph ye don't believe that I would be—"

"I don't know what I'd be believin', woman!" he shot back at her. Harriet, peeved, quickly closed the ring box and deposited it back on the table

"Joseph, ye mind yer mouth! We have a guest sleepin' in the cot, a young man."

"What? Another man! I canna leave ye by yerself for a minute afore ye'r at it again!"

"Joseph Dugan! The young man would be Henry McTavish. He came callin' for ye, not yer ever lovin' wife!"

At that moment, the guest in question appeared in the doorway to the kitchen.

"Pardon me, I'd be hopin' me presence wouldna be a problem. I'll be fetchin' me cap an' leavin'." Tavy headed to the table to retrieve the cap, lying next to the ring box.

"No for a minute! I asked ye to be sharin' supper wi' us and that ye'll be doin'," Harriet insisted.

"Henry McTavish? Pat McTavish's son?" Joseph's interest flared.

"Aye sir," Henry confirmed.

Joseph offered a welcoming hand, which the guest honored with a handshake. "Aye, Paddy brought ye board when ye were but seven or eight. That was the year, I married Mrs. Dugan." Joseph smiled at his wife, then immediately withdrew with a sneer and turned back to Tavy. "Henry, how is me ol' shipmate?"

"They call me Tavy, sir... Lost at sea, in the last storm."

Joseph stared helplessly at the floor in disbelief, then began pacing slowly.

"Ol' Paddy gone? I canna imagine. He survived two capsizin's and the wreck o' the Seamoor." Joseph turned away from his shipmate's son to conceal, the trembling of his lower lip.

"Sir, it was the worst we'd ever been through. Giant swells they were. First time in two years that he went out alone. I was sick wi' food poisonin'. Guess mother convinced the dear Lord that it wasna me time to be joinin' 'em."

Harriet entered the conversation, observing her husband's distraction. "Yes, laddie, we all have our time. Ye need that special lady first," Harriet added with a gentle pat to his back and a twinkle in her eye. The two watched Joseph fade into the parlor without any further comment, shocked by the news of the loss of his friend and still reeling from the possible infidelity of his wife. Harriet watched after her husband; she had witnessed the familiar response countless times. Losing a shipmate was losing a brother who fought along side in the struggle against Mother Nature.

Henry looked to Harriet for a cue.

"Henry let him be for a bit to grieve. In a few minutes you can present the coat. He'll be needin' it." In a short time Joseph returned to the kitchen.

"Yer father was one o' me dearest friends. Do him proud Henry McTavish." He turned to his wife, "I'll be puttin' Jock in for the night."

"Wait sir, I have somethin' for ye." Henry retrieved the coat from the back room with some apprehension and handed it to his father's dear friend. Recognizing the garment from the past, Joseph handled the coat ever so gently and nodded. After he slipped off his own weather beaten jacket, he put it on. Harriet walked over to latch the top brass clasp beneath his collar and then patted his chest.

"There ye be, perfect to keep out the cold." Joseph reached down to the table and with a swift move, removed the ring box from the table and dropped it into the coat pocket. Without expression, he looked into his wife's concerned eyes, then nodded at Tavy and left to attend to the mule.

Jock stopped grazing and looked attentively toward his master, anticipating its evening hay allotment, when, to its dismay, Joseph retrieved the harness from the shed. Within a few minutes, Jock was pulling the cart down the road to the cottage of Jon Wiggins. Upon arrival, Joseph showed the ring to his dearest friend. After a short heated dialogue, Joseph ignored Jon's advice, tightened his grasp on the odious ring box and set his destination for the home of his rival, Lucas McClurry of Brachney Hall.

He cracked the whip, his blood boiling, exasperated by the token of appreciation in his fist and further distressed by the loss of his shipmate. He drove Jock into a full trot, when the cart hit a loose plank on Erin MacBride Bridge. The board flipped up and caught in the axle, tipping the cart out of control. The ring box, once tight in the driver's hand was hurled into the stream below when he grasped the reins to pull the frightened mule to a halt. Joseph yelled, "Whoa!" as he too was thrown from his seat and landed in the dirt on his right shoulder. Jock stopped on command and Joseph let out a low groan as he sat up in the cloud of dust. After a short massage to his shoulder, he stood up and brushed some of the dirt from his clothing.

The darkness hindered the inspection of his vehicle, but he promptly determined that no damage was done. He uprighted the cart and shook his head in disappointment for his haste. He comforted the mule with a gentle pat and a few kind words for his immediate stop and then tightened the harness. He spent a few minutes looking for the ring box, which was nowhere to be found and climbed back into the cart. After regaining his bearings, he encouraged the mule to continue their mission to Brachney Hall.

Once at Lucas McClurry's home, Joseph rapped the doorknocker with a vengeance; every stroke sending a shooting pain to his injured shoulder. Armed with his magnifying glass, the master left the dining room table, strewn with loose stamps, and fled to the massive door of the front hall. He was astounded to greet the enraged face of Joseph Dugan, who abruptly demanded.

"Come out here young man and I'll be givin' ye ten seconds to explain why ye be givin' me wife that ring. Out here, man! It may be lost but that doesna let ye off the hook!" Edward lowered his glass and weakly complied.

"Sir, you lost *my* ring?" Edward was flabbergasted with the realization that the costly ring was now missing.

"Aye, and ye can be glad o' it! Have ye no ears? Ye have five seconds to explain why ye be givin' me wife that blasted ring!"

"Mr. Dugan?"

"Aye, and don't be denyin' it! Now answer me question and don't be lyin' to me, Lucas McClurry, or I willna show ye any mercy and break ye in half."

"Mr. Dugan," Edward swallowed hard, "I didn't give your wife the ring. Mrs. McDonnally gave it to her accidentally... with the mending. Sir, you have nothing to worry about, I am not attracted to your wife in the slightest," Edward affirmed with a thin smile.

"And why would that be? Do ye find something undesirable in me wife's appearance?" the offended spouse charged.

"No, no sir, Mrs. Dugan is a lovely woman."

"Aye, and ye wouldna be the first wantin' Harriet for himself!"

"No, no, sir...I am a married man!"

"Aye? Then where be ye wife?"

"No, I meant to say, that I am going to be married," Edward recovered quickly, struggling with each leading remark. Edward relented with no other alternative and invited the disgruntled spouse into his home for further explanation. "Please calm down, and come in Mr. Dugan."

Once inside, Edward led Joseph to the parlor. The lighted room, revealed two truths: first, Edward discovered that his guest was still covered in the elements of the road and second, Joseph realized that Lucas McClurry looked oh so familiar. Joseph spoke first.

"Edward McDonnally? I thought ye had joined ye Maker," astonished, Joseph struggled to imagine the face beyond the beard.

"Yes, Joseph. I apologize for this misunderstanding. That ring has caused me nearly more trouble than my worst enemy." Joseph reached out with a handshake for the truce and a friendly welcome to his old acquaintance.

"Why would ye be charadin' as McClurry? Trouble wi' the law?"

"No, Joseph. It's a long story... about eighteen years long."

"Sorry about the ring. 'Twas pulled from me hand in the accident."

"An accident? Are you injured?" Edward inquired with concern.

"No, only me pride. I will go look for yer ring."

"I'll go with you, I'll fetch two lanterns."

"If ye have a hammer and nails, we would be needin' them too. A plank's off o' the bridge."

The two men checked the area near the bridge, but failed to recover the lost box. They made a quick repair to the bridge and returned to Brachney Hall where the two men talked openly. Edward treated his friend to his very first hot cup of chocolate malted drink and provided Jock with a flake of hay.

"How is Harriet, going to take to the news of the missing ring, Joseph?"

"'Twasn't hers to start wi'. Ne'er ye mind. I'll be handlin' Harriet. She's in for a surprise to find ye bein' Edward McDonnally," Joseph chuckled while Edward led him to the door.

"I'll see you both at the St. Andrew's celebration."

"Aye," Joseph agreed, as he untied Jock to begin his trip back to the cottage.

Edward had given Joseph the details of the misadventures with the engagement ring. Even though Joseph had found them to be thoroughly entertaining, he had vowed to keep the conversation confidential. Mr. Dugan's light-hearted reaction to the tales had given Edward a new perspective on the subject, believing that he had taken the miscommunications and value of the ring much too seriously. The loss of the ring manifested a breeze of relief that blew a hole in the tangled web of deception. Edward crawled out to enjoy momentary freedom from *his* troubles as he bid farewell to Joseph, waving in the moonlit road.

Chapter XI

"St. Andrew's Day"

I never saw so sweet a face
As that I stood before:
My heart has left its dwelling place
And can return no more.

—John Clare

With the discovery that Tavy had a full week available before he would return to his ship, the Dugans generously invited him to reside with them at their cottage. The young sailor gratefully accepted their invitation and quickly developed a special relationship with the couple. Angel became his walking companion, much like the mutt he had as a lad. Tavy spent the next few evenings submerged in seafaring adventures provided by the veteran, Joseph. During daylight hours, the young guest helped Joseph repair the drystone dykes that marked the field boundaries and assisted in replacing the cobblestones with pipeclay designed flagstones at the cottage doorstep.

Tavy became the son that Harriet never had and enjoyed his company immensely, however her motherly instincts encouraged her to remedy the young visitor's social life. The invitation to the November thirtieth St. Andrew's Day celebration at the McDonnally mansion that evening provided the ideal opportunity to introduce Tavy to some of Lochmoor's younger generation.

At the manor, the guests would be soon arriving, donning their Scottish attire and merry-making dispositions. Hiram entered the kitchen to make a final check with Eloise to insure that the refreshments were plentiful and then graciously helped load the dumbwaiter. He exited to the dining room to retrieve his late Grandmother Selrach's silver bowl for the chocolate candies that he had requested a Swiss friend to ship as a special treat for his guests. There he found Allison, dressed beautifully in lavender, sorting through the linens, in search of an additional tablecloth.

"Good evening, Allison."

Allison looked up from the drawer, "Good evening."

"I trust you are well."

"Very well, in fact. Thanks to your hospitality, I have been enjoying this visit with my mother...immensely."

"And Mr. Zigmann?" he teased, while he lifted the silver bowl from the looming cherry hutch.

"Albert?" she questioned keenly, refolding the cloth.

"Yes, how is Albert...and of course, his fine son, Guillaume?" he asked nonchalantly as he emptied the box of chocolates into the bowl.

"Both are quite well, I am sure. You can see for yourself. They *are* up in the ballroom, as you know," she returned the smile and closed the drawer.

Hiram's fishing trip was a success, obvious by Allison's subtle, but positive demeanor.

"Guillaume is a very fortunate man."

Allison cocked her head slightly with an expression of 'do you really think so?'

Hiram read her thoughts.

She thanked him and returned to the third floor. Hiram stood for a moment with thoughts of life's unexpected turn of events; first his relationship with Allison, secondly with his seemingly fruitless search for his twin. He moved to the large mirror above the buffet and looked at the image before him.

Well, Hiram, old man, what are you going to do if you do find her? How will you prove to her that she is Hannah? He looked deep into the dark eyes reflecting back when with the swiftness of an arrow, the answer came to him. He delivered the bowl of chocolates to Eloise who positioned it in the dumbwaiter and pulled it up to Albert in the ballroom. Then, in a near sprint, he shot to the third floor.

After considerable preparation at the Dugan cottage, Harriet made a final once over of Joseph and Tavy. While combing Tavy's hair, she remarked, "Imagine that, Lucas McClurry bein' none other than Edward McDonnally. Wait 'til I see him. And mind ye, me dearest friend in the world, Eloise Zigmann, no sayin' a word about it to me; she'll be catchin' it for that!"

"Now, Harriet, ye heard what I be warnin'. Everyone was sworn to secrecy."

"Ye ne'er told me what happened to me precious jewel," she pouted.

"Harriet, ye'll be not aggravating the guests at the party, o' we willna be attendin' it."

"Verra well, I'll do me best," Harriet complied tapping the comb on her palm.

"Now Harriet, would ye be kind enough to fetch me pocket watch from me drawer. I would be needin' to speak privately wi' the boy."

"Aye, helpless men ye are. Straighten ye kilt." Joseph winked at Tavy as they watched Harriet enter the bedroom. Harriet opened the top drawer, let out a squeal of delight and rushed back to the parlor.

"Joseph, ye wonderful man! It is the most beautiful ring I ever laid me eyes on!" she hugged her husband, clutching the black satin covered box. "Place it on me finger, Joseph," Harriet asked, smiling up at the two very pleased men.

"It's a bit smaller and has but one wee emerald. But it comes wi' a great deal more love than the lost ring, Harriet," Joseph assured, placing the silver ring on Harriet's finger. A tear formed in the corner of the grateful wife's eye as she reached up and kissed her husband of many years. Tavy dropped his head to lend the loving couple some privacy.

Harriet proudly marched her well-groomed men down the road to the manor, with Angel trailing close behind. The Dugan's arrived with time to spare.

Meanwhile, the Master of McDonnally Manor was turning the silver key, with the green tassel, in the lock of the door to his mother's room, a few doors down from the bustling ballroom. Unlike Naomi, he had no qualms about entering the room. The oil lamp that he had lifted from the hall table lit his path to the dressing table. He paused to lose himself in the reminiscent rosewater scent, observing the four poster bed beautifully draped in feminine linens. He remembered his mother speaking like it was only yesterday.

Hiram, my sweet son, don't be afraid, I will be fine. It is you that I worry about. You must be a good little soldier and stay with your grandmother till your father returns. You will never be alone, Edward will be there too.

Never alone? he thought. *Elizabeth, I need to get back to her.*

He hurried over to the writing table and smiled proudly at the portrait of his mother. He held the lamp close to her face. *You were a beauti-*

ful woman, Mother. Such a pity you can't join us to-night.

The lamp flickered as he directed his steps to the dressing table. Without a moment's hesitation he opened the drawer in the dressing table and held the lamp near it, while his large hand slid to the back where his fingers closed around a floral handkerchief folded in a small square. He pulled the treasure into view, sat the lamp on the table and placed the small bundle in his left palm and slowly unwrapped it with his right. He dropped down to the bench before the table and breathed deeply. This was the answer; he was certain of it. He held the golden locket up to the light for closer examination.

Yes, Mother. I will find her. If she were dead I would feel it. He removed his white silk handkerchief from his vest pocket and wrapped the locket and then placed it in his pocket. After reverently refolding the floral hankie and replacing it in the drawer, he was mentally prepared to leave when a final glimpse at his mother's serene smile detained him.

Allison had returned to the kitchen and was snitching from the sweet tray when the door knocker sounded. Eloise wiped her hands on the embroidered tea towel and slipped past Allison to receive the guests. A whiff of slightly burned haggis drew her frantically back to the kitchen; after which, Allison relieved Eloise from her welcoming duties and scurried down the hall to unlatch the main door.

"Good evenin', Allison! Take a gander at me gorgeous ring!"

"Mrs. Dugan, it's lovely," Allison yielded with hesitation, expecting to see the elaborate ring from Edward.

"'Tis a gift from me everlovin' husband." Harriet patted Joseph, now wearing a sheepish grin. "And this fine lad is Henry McTavish. Like a son he is. Hope you dunna mind another guest. Tavy's been stayin' with Mr. Dugan and meself at the cottage for a wee bit afore he returns to sea. His father was a dear friend of Joseph's, Patrick McTavish. Poor man, lost in a storm, he was."

"Sorry, Henry."

"He prefers Tavy," Harriet insisted.

"Welcome, Tavy and good evening Mr. Dugan."

The young man stood motionless, in awe of the breathtaking hostess. Her angelic face sent a chill through his spine. She was, indeed, the most beautiful woman he had ever met.

Joseph spoke up, "Good evenin', Miss Allison, ye'r lookin' lovely. Would Jon Wiggins be present as yet?"

Harriet cut in, "Be present as yet? Can't ye live one day wi'out that ...that butcher!"

"Not a truer friend lived, Harriet."

"Mr. Wiggins is upstairs, but I must alert you that he is in the company of a woman."

"Aye, Jon Wiggins escorting a female companion? I thought I'd ne'r live to see the day," Harriet remarked. Her husband scowled with disapproval and disappointment; first for the depressing outlook for the evening without the full attention of his best friend, secondly for Jon's secrecy of the relationship.

"Weel, Joseph, it appears that ye wouldna be the only one wi' secrets. Ye may have to devote yer attention to ye spouse for a change." Harriet smiled victoriously and proceeded through the portal to the ballroom with her husband lagging behind. "Come along, Joseph, I have to show off me jewel to Eloise," she commanded.

The couple continued up the staircase leaving their guest at the portal. Upon reaching the ballroom, Harriet left Joseph and set out on a mission to locate Edward, who had revealed his identity to the other guests, only a few minutes earlier. She found him speaking with Bruce Wheaton. The two men were discussing the archaeological find of the fifty –thousand year old Piltdown Man, near Lewes, the previous year. Harriet didn't hesitate to interrupt the conversation.

"Aye, Edward McDonnally, it has been awhile." Edward, standing with his arms folded turned to the familiar voice asking, "Lucas McClurry, might I have a word wi' ye?"

Edward's look of surprise melted into a pleasant grin. "Hello, Harriet. Excuse me, Bruce. It's nice to see you Mrs. Dugan."

Harriet cocked her head slightly to the right to examine his face. "Aye, the whiskers play tricks on me eyes... 'tis you, Edward McDonnally. Welcome back," she offered with a warm hug. "Mr. Dugan, n'er meant to lose me ring, but I do thank ye. 'Twas verra beautiful, but between ye and me," she leaned closer, "Joseph wasna too pleased. Look at the beauty me husband gave me." Harriet extended her hand before him.

"It's lovely. Your husband is a remarkable man."

"No a better man lives. Now I must find Eloise." She scurried through the crowd. She stopped immediately, when she noticed the beautiful Elizabeth and proceeded to interrogate the unsuspecting guest, and show off her latest acquisition.

In the main hall, Allison introduced herself to the Dugans' houseguest.

"Tavy, I'm Allison O'Connor; wouldn't you like to come in?" Allison offered. He stared at her, enchanted by her glistening blonde hair that dropped around her dainty shoulders, but did not reply, thinking, *she's a living porcelain doll.*

Allison locked onto Tavy's arm and escorted him over the threshold, giggling, "C'mon, sailor. Forget the sea for awhile and join the landlubbers!"

The pair sauntered into the hall, coming face to face with Allison's slightly taken aback significant other. Tall and slender, Guillaume stood somber and notably concerned, sizing up Allison's well-built escort.

"Guillaume, look what we have here, a sea-lovin' individual who is as quiet as a church mouse. How uncommon wouldn't you think? Not at all like Captain Dugan," Allison provoked.

"Captain Dugan?" Henry spoke up.

"Ah, he can speak; I was testing your vocal abilities. Needless to say, I'm certain Mr. Dugan would have made a mighty fine captain had he not left the sea. Tavy this is Guillaume Zigmann. His parents are caretakers of McDonnally Manor."

Why didn't you introduce me as your beau to the sea rat? Guillaume searched her face curiously with disapproval then thrust his right hand toward the handsome rival when, his adversary questioned."

"Aye? A servant here in this fine house?" Tavy reached to follow through with the greeting when Guillame, although driven to withdraw from the intruder's intimidating powerful grip, remained steadfast without retreat.

Allison felt the tension between the two growing and intervened, "Tavy is Mr. and Mrs. Dugan's guest." While the two locked glares, Allison continued, uneasily, "He is the son of Mr. Dugan's shipmate." Allison latched on to the arms of the two young men.

"C'mon men, let's join the other guests!" Allison suggested, wedged between the two sparring males. For Guillaume, the journey to the third floor was infinitely long. With each entertaining word that *his* girl directed to the new guest, he felt a strike to his relationship with her. The lively music drifting down the stairs, riddled with Tavy's unbridled laughter set a nauseating ambiance that further irritated the already livid rival. The triangle reached the ballroom entrance, still attached, with neither male relenting to the either.

Naomi spotted the threesome and immediately excused herself from her conversation with the postman, Mr. Kilvert, to inform Hiram of their arrival. However, the host was nowhere to be found. She made a quick inquiry with Elizabeth and Edward to his whereabouts, but neither had any information. She then asked the Wheatons, recalling that she had seen Hiram holding their newest family member, which had sparked images of the search for Hannah.

With no sign of Hiram, she moved through the crowd. Upon reaching her daughter and her escorts, she warmly greeted the new face.

"Welcome, I am Allison's mother, Naomi McDonnally. Harriet and Joseph have spoken so highly of you," she smiled pleasantly.

Henry McTavish's jovial face turned scarlet, fixed on the hideous scar running down Naomi's. He dropped Allison's arm and slowly edged backward, breathing heavier. He then broke quickly for the stairs.

His unexpected flight left Naomi and daughter stunned. Guillaume, on the other hand, read Tavy's actions as intolerably deplorable. His defensive instincts took hold, armed to attack the culprit who had dishonored and embarrassed not only one of his dearest friends, but his future mother-in-law. Feeling no sympathy, only contempt, he took out after Tavy.

"No, Guillaume!" Naomi pleaded, but he had disappeared down the staircase out of earshot.

The fiddling stopped and silence befell the ballroom. Naomi turned to her daughter, as the crowd gradually resumed conversing and the music restored.

"I have dealt with the typical unpleasant reponses, but, his was considerably more severe. I think that he was seeing more than my damaged face."

"Mother, I'm worried about them, neither was civil to the other since they met downstairs."

Harriet appeared asking, "Where's Tavy?"

"Harriet, he left quite upset, immediately after he met me. I'm afraid that he was terribly disturbed by my scar."

"So sorry, Mrs. McDonnally. Aye... I have an idea what happened. I need to fetch him. I'll be explainin' later." Harriet headed hastily to the staircase.

"Harriet, wait!" Naomi called.

"What is it, Mrs. McDonnally?"

"Guillaume was outraged and has gone to find him."

"Oh, mercy!"

"Maybe I should send Edward, or Joseph."

"No, I'll handle it, dunna be worryin'!" With that, Harriet descended the stairs, as quickly as her stout legs could carry her. Harriet reached the main entrance and rushed outside.

In the meantime, Guillaume caught up with Tavy just as he was entering the oak woods between McDonnally Manor and Brachney Hall. Guillaume grasped Tavy's left arm stopping him in his tracks. Fearless and without reservation to the imposing size of the offender, Guillaume jerked Tavy around, reprimanding, "How dare you! Who do you think you are? Naomi McDonnally is a saint!" Tavy remained in his grasp with apparently no objection.

"She would never hurt a single soul. I should drop you right here!" Guillaume threatened pulling Tavy into his face by way of his coat lapels.

Harriet flew out of the darkness, arms waving, "No, Guillaume, no, dunna hurt'im! Ye dunna understand!"

Out of respect for Mrs. Dugan, he loosened his grip, then gave Tavy a shove to his chest.

"Laddie, listen to me. Tavy meant no harm to Mrs. McDonally. I'm certain o' that."

Tavy dropped his head from Guillaume's piercing scrutiny.

"Guillaume, please come wi' me," she insisted. He left his adversary defiantly and then followed Harriet down the road to the portal.

"Come in where 'tis warm wi' me, Guillaume, I'm about to catch me death."

Harriet opened the heavy door to the main hall. Guillaume followed Harriet into the study where she politely shooed out Jake Kilvert and his intended, Agnes. Once Guillaume was safely inside, Harriet closed the pocket doors.

"Guillaume, yer defendin' Mrs, McDonnally is honorable, I wunna be disagreein' wi' that." Guillaume stood rocking slightly with his arms folded across his chest, listening respectfully. "Tavy, was tak'in by surprise. It wasna Mrs. McDonnally's scar that shocked him. 'Twas the scar— a scar like the one Tavy's mother suffered when she was murdered on the docks."

"Murdered?" Guillaume said under his breath.

"Aye, died at the hands of drunkards. Tavy, acted wi'out thinkin'."

Guillaume, sighed, "Yes, Mrs. Dugan, as I did. I'll talk to him. Naomi needs you now. I know her, she's not at all concerned about herself, but with us. Tell her that all is well."

"Yer a good man, Guillaume Zigmann. But what else would Eloise and Albert have?" Harriet smiled as she gave Guillaume a motherly hug, then left the study to find Naomi.

Guillaume pulled up his collar and opened the main door to find Tavy sitting in the portal.

Tavy spoke first, "I ne'r meant to disrespect Allison's mother... me mother—"

Guillaume sympathetically cut him off, "No need. Mrs. Dugan explained. The proper thing to do now is to go back upstairs and face Mrs. McDonnally with a smile. She is one of my closest friends. She wants for nothing more than for you to be comfortable, so that you can join the others for the celebration." Tavy sat staring at his boots.

"I'll be upstairs," Guillaume added, then entered the hall.

"Guillaume, thank ye."

Guillaume nodded; Tavy followed him to the ballroom. Hiram returned to the party after a short prayer in his mother's memory. He welcomed the young sailor and introduced him to the other guests congregating in the ballroom. Before too long, Tavy was conversing freely, but chose to keep his distance from the captivating Miss O'Connor, out of respect for the his honorable peer, Mr. Zigmann.

St. Andrew, patron saint of Scotland would have been pleased to find the guests blissfully celebrating his honored day, as would, Hiram's mother, Amanda McDonnally.

Allison kept her promise to save all her dances for Guillaume, who spent a good part of his evening, when not on the dance floor, chatting with Edward. Elizabeth was engaged in a lengthy discussion with Helen Kilvert who was scheduled to visit the Louvre in the spring and had a number of suggestions for Elizabeth's storefront. Harriet Dugan found, to her surprise, that Jon Wiggins' date, Mildred from Devonshire, was quite agreeable, leaving Joseph and Jon to creating tall tales for the children, who found the two pups decidedly more entertaining. Eloise, being partial to infants, assisted Maryanne with the new baby giving the young mother a free evening with her husband.

Albert provided the majority of the music, and accompanied a little ditty presented by Lochmoor's seafaring visitor. The highlight of the evening was Mr. Dugan's heart rendering performance on the bagpipes which brought tears to all in attendance and unmatched pride to his wife.

The party continued into the wee hours of the morning and was remembered as one of the most pleasurable of all St. Andrew's Day celebration in Lochmoor.

Chapter XII

"The Sister"

Warm summer sun,
Shine kindly here.
Warm southern wind,
Blow softly here.

Green sod above,
Lie light,lie light.
Good night, dear heart,
Good night, good night.

—Mark Twain

As the weeks passed, Naomi and Hiram worked on several leads in the search for Hannah. To their dismay, their findings reached a dead end. They decided to give up the search and concentrate on their personal matters. Hiram returned to London and Naomi spent her spare time finalizing the details for the Burns' Night preparation.

Early in January, Naomi went to the village mercantile to purchase brightly colored fabric for bunting to decorate Brachney Hall. She entered the shop to find that she was the sole customer and proceeded to examine the bolts of material at her leisure. Within a few minutes Naomi's quiet shopping ended with the elevated voice of the clerk, her stepmother, Dagmar. It wasn't long before the quarrelling partner in the heated dispute was revealed to be Naomi's insufferable father, Nathan MacKenzie. Naomi moved quickly behind the towering bolts of tweed, to listen as the approaching voices grew louder.

"Grimvald is my home too! I vill look in any drawer I vant!" The irate Swede continued to lash her defiant husband with her sharp tongue. "Nat'an, answer me!! Who is dis Vila?! Come back here!!" she bellowed.

Vila, Hiram and Hannah's nanny? My father knew Vila? Naomi clenched the bolt of satin, shocked by the timely exchange.

"Nat'an, you tell me, *now*! Vy vere you sending dis voman all dis money?!" Dagmar insisted.

"Woman, I warned ye to be keepin' yer hands out o' me desk!! For yer information, she was me son's Nanny when his useless mother abandoned him!" Nathan retaliated.

This derogatory comment sent Naomi's adrenalin pumping to her quavering limbs. It took every ounce of restraint for Naomi to remain concealed from view. Her brain was flooded with dates and a series of events.

How dare you speak that way about mother! You forced her to leave Jeremiah! She left to protect me from your drunken rages! Wait one minute! Vila kidnapped Hannah a year before Jeremiah was born. Did she come back?

She knew that Vila was not at Grimwald while she was there with her mother. She also had no knowledge of the events at Grimwald after she and her mother moved to Newcastle.

You knew Vila and she kidnapped Hannah. Did you and Vila hide Hannah at Grimwald when Jeremiah was an infant? Naomi questioned with horror.

Naomi motivated by the injustice and seeking to unravel the mystery moved from the shadows while viewing the bickering couple. With sight of his threatening daughter's face, aware that she had witnessed the convicting conflict, Nathan immediately fled through the back exit.

"STOP HIM!" Naomi screeched, her hands trembling, her face flushed with contempt.

The shock of Naomi's presence all but silenced Dagmar as she approached the enraged stepdaughter.

"Naomi. Dis is not your business," Dagmar scowled.

Naomi brushed past her aggravated stepmother toward the window of the back door. With only a trail of dust lingering from the speeding cart,

Naomi returned to interrogate Dagmar about the woman and the monies dispersed.

"Dagmar, I need to know, is the woman's name Vila Ramsey?" Naomi asked in haste.

"Yah, it is. Vhat do you know about dis Vila? Natan vas afraid ven he saw you. Vhat is your quarrel vit' him?"

"And what is my father's connection with her?" Naomi demanded ignoring the opportunity to explain the myriad of personal problems that she had with her father.

"Veren't you listening? I vould like to know too!" Dagmar retorted.

"I'm sorry Dagmar." Naomi backed down. "We both need answers, but we can work together on this and time is of the essence. I need the evidence, the information you spoke of. I am certain that if we don't move expeditiously, Nathan will destroy it!"

"I dun't need de evidence. I have seen enough," the betrayed wife wiped her hands on her apron, raised her head high and walked behind the counter. She began rearranging the Bavarian music boxes on the large white doily.

"You don't understand, I need to know if there were receipts?" Naomi asked desperately.

"Dun't raise your voice to me young voman! Of course dere vere receipts, dat's how I found out," Dagmar remarked, incensed at Naomi.

"He will destroy them, if we don't hurry to Grimwald!" Naomi warned.

"Vhy should I care? I need no more proof; Nat'an has no respect for me."

"Dagmar, was there an address?" Naomi begged.

"Who is dis Vila? Who is she to you?"

"I'll explain later, Dagmar, I realize that we are not well acquainted but this is urgent. Trust me. You are a mother and you adore your children. A child's life is at stake!"

"Vat are you saying?' Dagmar asked, disturbed by her stepdaughter's fearful tone.

"All right, Dagmar," Naomi relented. "There is something that you need to know about Nathan. I know this will not be something that you want to hear, but the evidence is leading to the distinct possibility that your husband has done something despicable, criminal in fact."

Naomi realized that her stepmother's opinion of Nathan was clouded and she needed to speak carefully if she was to gain Dagmar's allegiance. Although Nathan had never been anything but loathsome in Naomi's eyes, the fact remained that Dagmar had married him.

"Dagmar, you, more than anyone are entitled to this information. It is common knowledge that this woman, Vila Ramsey, was a nanny for the McDonnally family the year before I was born. When the McDonnally twins, Hiram and Hannah were two years of age, she kidnapped the little girl. A year later, my mother and I left Grimwald. It seems fantastic to imagine, but Vila could have secretly returned to Lochmoor with Hannah that year. She may have been a nanny for my newborn brother at Grimwald. No one would be the wiser; no one ever visited Grimwald. If no one was aware of my father's relationship with Vila, he would have never been suspected as an accomplice."

"Nat'an has been helping dis kidnapper?"

"Yes, Dagmar. He hated the McDonnally clan. Probably still does."

Dagmar moved the largest of the three brightly orange painted Dala Horses, in front of the other two. She left the counter distraught and disillusioned, then sank down to the bench situated near the shelves of boots. Naomi looked on with a sudden surge of guilt as the bearer of ill-tidings and compassionately slid a comforting arm around Dagmar's strong shoulders.

"I'm sorry, you are a good woman, Dagmar. You don't need to be shackled to one as disreputable as my father. When I met you, I had hoped that you would be a savior to his redemption, but as I said, his act was a criminal offense." Naomi knelt in front of Dagmar and pleaded, "I beg you, Dagmar, do you remember an address connected with this woman. Was there any correspondence?"

"Vone does not easily forget ver vone vas born," Dagmar offered solemnly.

Naomi squinted as she deciphered the comment, "Sweden?"

"Stockholm. Vonce a year Nat'an agreed to take me home to visit my shildren. He vas happy to do dis. How generous of him." The words flowed through her lips with the melancholy of a funeral march while she studied the worn braided rug beneath her tan scuffed clogs.

As always, Naomi was shamed and disgusted by her father's manipulative plans. Her elation for the information was deflated by her observation of her depressed stepmother.

"Vas dis nanny married?" Dagmar inquired, refusing to speak the name of her husband's accomplice and possible lover.

"Not at the time of her service. She resided in the McDonnally home."

"I didn't tink so, "Dagmar added without reservation. There was a moment of silence, which was followed by Dagmar's confession.

"After I lost my first husband, I didn't vant to marry again. De shildren ver small and dey vould have never approved. But as dey grew up and left home, vone by vone, I vas lonely and tired. I t'ought Nat'an vas too. Tired he vas. Lonely, I doubt....So he helped dis voman kidnap de little McDonnally girl? De poor missus, she must have been beside herself vith vorry, I can't imagine my babies being stolen from der beds...Vhy did he hate dis family so much to du someting so horrible?"

"It was an ongoing land dispute. Nathan believed that a large portion of McDonnally Manor was his, "Naomi explained.

"Is he not right in de head?"

"Well, disturbed at the very least, Dagmar."

"Nat'an is a private man. I am sure dat dere are many t'ings dat I dun't know about him. I vas surprised vit' him mourning your sister, his annual vigil to her grave,"

"Sister? I have no sister," Naomi replied with shock. Dagmar was equally taken aback.

"He says it vas his dau'ter. Vas it not your moders shild? Did he marry again after your moder?"

"No, you were the first, after mother as far as I know... What is the name of this daughter?"

"Natalia, after him, I believe."

"When did she pass?" Naomi's interest increased with each answer her stepmother provided.

"As a baby, many, many years ago."

"You said that he visits her grave? Where?"

"At Grimvald, in de voods, on de nort' side of de land."

"Dagmar, I've been in those woods dozens of times, since I returned to Grimwald after I lost my mother. There was never a grave site. I need to see the headstone. Please, close the shop and accompany me to Grimwald. You need to know too," Naomi urged.

"I dun't know if dat is a good idea. Nat'an is as angry as a raging bull. He saw how upset you vere. And I can't leave, I am in charge of de shop. The owner vould not like it."

"Please, Dagmar, I'll deal with Nathan and you can explain to Mr. Galt that it was a family emergency. Besides, there are no customers here. My cart is outside, we can take it."

"Good, den. I'll lock up." Dagmar pulled the shade on the door, turned the sign in the window and pulled on her overcoat, with Naomi's help. The two women left through the backdoor and while Dagmar climbed to her seat, Naomi untied the horse and then took her place next to her stepmother. With a clicking and a jiggling of the reins the chestnut horse broke into a trot across the cobblestones.

"Dis is unnerving me, Naomi, and I dun't frighten easily."

"I know...get up laddie!" she commanded the graceful horse to quicken its pace.

"Dagmar, what did my father tell you about this child?"

"Not'ing, I found out on my own. Ven ve first married and returned to Grimvald, I saw him leaving de barn von morning, heading for de voods with a handful of flowers." Dagmar continued, "He returned several minutes later, empty-handed and began his vork in de fields. Later dat afternoon, ven he rode to de village, I followed de path tru the voods." Naomi edged closer to listen, now impeded by the wind whipping through the cart. *My father showing something other than anger and contempt?* Naomi thought.

"In a small clearing, left of de path stood a small headstone vit' the name Natalia MacKenzie. I remember my heart sinking vhen I discovered dat she passed de same year ven she vas born. I felt dat I had violated Natan's privacy, den I felt disappointed dat he vould not share somet'ing so important wit' me as dis."

Did I really have a sister? Or could this be Hannah? Naomi wondered, not quite sure if she could cope with either conclusion.

"Naomi, vhat are you tinking?" Dagmar queried reluctantly, raising her voice over the whipping winds.

"Dagmar, I don't know what to think. I'll know after I see the dates on the headstone, Naomi shouted." The two women faced forward silently pressing their way through the crisp January air. Naomi gently snapped the reins to hasten her steed. She poured over the details of the last hours. Her mystery solving mind was working overtime, yet the pieces were not falling easily into place.

As the woods on the Grimwald estate came into view over the last hill, Naomi announced "I'm going to take the back entrance to the woods. After I check the dates we'll go up to the house." With the old iron gate looming before them, Naomi halted the horse.

"I should have asked Nat'an about his dau'ter," Dagmar said regretfully.

"Like you said, he is a very private man. He may not have confided in you, even if you had. You stay here Dagmar, and try to keep warm. I'll go alone," she insisted handing a woolen tartan blanket from behind the seat. Naomi retied her scarf and jumped down from the cart. She tied the horse to the fence and headed to the gate. Her fingers worked at the gate latch, coated in decades of rust, but were unsuccessful in freeing it from its frozen state. She gathered her skirt after several minutes of frustration and proceeded to climb the cold irons. She threw a victorious wave to Dagmar as she headed toward the only path with which she was familiar. Dagmar snuggled down beneath the blanket, still stewing in her newfound misery.

Naomi stepped quickly, following traces of the path. Her heart's pace increased with each crunching step that shattered the leaves beneath her boots. Midway into the woods she searched to the left then, to the right of the path. The pounding in her ears grew louder. Nothing, nothing... then there it appeared before her, the tiny mysterious headstone. She stared at the back of the grave marker and then took a deep breath, closed her eyes momentarily and prayed that the dates would not reveal her greatest fear- the possibility of this being the tomb of Hannah McDonnally.

Hiram and Hannah were born in 1878. She was kidnapped in1880, she mentally reviewed.

She edged her way to the face of the slab as her eyes raced to the dates beneath the scrolled engraved letters:

NATALIA MACKENZIE
Born
Tenth of May, 1875.

Received in Heaven
Fifteenth of March, 1876

Naomi's heart skipped a beat. She knew the memorial existed, she believed Dagmar without a second thought, yet seeing it produced a gut wrenching response.

"1876...she died two years before Hannah was born."

Naomi rechecked the dates. With a mental sigh of relief, she knelt down by the bittersweet discovery with melancholy respect for the sister she never knew.

"My sister? My older sister. Oh Natalia, who was your mother?"

Mother didn't know Nathan then. She removed her right glove. A cold chill ran through her fingers as she ran them over the curvature of the tablet and then fell anxiously down to the elaborate lettering.

"What happened to you Natalia?" She withdrew her trembling hand and took one last look at the weathered stone.

"Goodbye, sister. I'll see you in the next life." She kissed her index finger and placed it gently on the letter "N" that she shared with the unknown sibling. Naomi brushed the leaves from her skirt and hurried back to the cart. Dagmar raised her head when Naomi climbed into the cart next to her.

"It is not Hannah's grave. Natalia was born and passed prior to the kidnapping. She *was* my sister. Nathan must have marked the grave sometime after I left Grimwald, when I was sixteen. I wouldn't presume to know why. I choose not to believe that the dates are falsified, but rather that because Natalia was conceived out of wedlock. He didn't want my brother or I to discover the grave. I'm frankly surprised that he acknowledged her existence, let alone honor her with visits. There may be another side to my father that I wasn't aware of, perhaps, the one that led you to marry him," she looked sympathetically toward her passenger. Dagmar remained dubious about returning to the Grimwald House.

"We have to confront him, Dagmar. We have to find Vila, if we are ever to find Hannah. Hiram is looking for her and we may be able to help him." The horse made the swift curve in the back road with ease when Naomi asked. "Dagmar, are you prepared for this?"

"I'm not vone to dvell on troubles. Hurry, maybe he's still dere." With that cue, Naomi urged the horse back to the main road which connected to the lane leading to the house on the large estate.

As the little cart approached the large stone mansion, Naomi cringed with childhood memories advancing on her like the fires of Hades. She shook off the debilitating recollections and aided Dagmar as she stepped from the cart. Dagmar tried the door, only to find it locked. With Naomi's nod of approval, she placed the key from her pocketbook into the lock. The two stepped in and within a split second, Dagmar bellowed, "Nat'an! Nat'an!" startling Naomi.

The two women standing at the entry to the study simultaneously noticed that the desk had been ransacked. Not a word passed between them. Dagmar moved slowly toward the back of the hall and drew aside the lace curtain of the window. She stood viewing the vacant drive, her anger dissolving, being replaced with a sense of loss and loneliness. She sat down on the cobbler's bench in the hall and folded her hands in her lap.

"He's gone...I'm alone again," Dagmar muttered. Naomi looked on helplessly. "I don't know vhy I'm surprised...I should be happy."

"He wouldn't have left if he wasn't guilty, Dagmar," Naomi added cautiously.

"I know. Vat should I do? I really dun't vant to return to Sveden. Lochmoor and Grimvald have been my home for many years. I like my yob and my friends in the village."

"Of course you do. You have made Grimwald into a wonderful, pleasant home. I know that the village appreciates your excellent service at the store and everyone enjoys your company."

"Tank you," Dagmar sighed again.

"You stay here, this is your home. Nathan can't afford to return. He knows that I know too much and will notify the authorities. Dagmar, we have no evidence to his involvement now. I'm sure that he has taken everything that connects him with Vila."

"Yah, but you may find her in Sveden and maybe dis Hannah," Dagmar dried her eyes.

"Yes, I need to get back and tell Hiram to make contact with Stockholm to begin the search. I wonder if Jeremiah has any memories of Vila."

"Yeremiah dun't speak vit his fader either."

"Exactly, and for that very reason, he might have a few distasteful memories that he may care to share. Do you remember any dates when the letters were posted?"

"Only vone, six mont's ago. Tat's vy I vas upset. I feel dat he's tainted my homeland...both of dem."

"I see you kept the ink drawing," Naomi motioned to the frame above Dagmar's head. It was an ink drawing of two young girls gathering kindling. "I've always liked it. When I came back to Grimwald, I had a vague recollection of it from when I was very young. They say you can't remember incidents at such an early age, but it was so familiar to me. Later I pretended that it was a sketch of my ...." Naomi stopped abruptly.

"You and your sister?"

"Strange, isn't it Dagmar. I imagined I had a sister and I really did."

"I imagined dat I had a husband dat loved me... imagined."

"Dagmar, do you want me to take you back to the store?"

"No, tank you. I must clean up dis mess." Dagmar removed her outerwear and showed Naomi to the door. Looking into her stepdaughter's concerned eyes, Dagmar half-smiled and arranged the loosened scarf around Naomi's head.

"I'll be fine. Dere isn't a man alive dat can blow out my spark for life!" They hugged as Naomi insisted that Dagmar contact her if she needed anything or someone to talk to.

Naomi reached in her coat pockets for her gloves, noticing that she had only one, not realizing that the other remained with her sister.

Naomi returned to Lochmoor in record time. Each crack of the whip brought her closer to that moment of truth when she'd share the information with Hiram. She parked the cart in front of the telegraph office and tied the horse to the worn hitching post. Naomi gathered her skirt and stepped down from the cart and hurried into the office nearly knocking over Mrs. Innes, who was on her way out. After a short apology, she greeted the telegrapher "Hello, Mr. Graham, I need to send a telegram immediately."

"I'm ready, when yer ready, Mrs. McDonnally."

"This has to be kept in the strictest confidence, Mr. Graham."

"But o'course, proceed when yer ready."

"I have found VR. STOP Nathan is funding in Stockholm STOP He has left, aware that I know this STOP Godspeed STOP

Chapter XIII

"Another Web"

His heart in me,
keeps me and him in one,
My heart in him,
his thoughts and senses guides:
He loves my heart,
for once it was his own:
I cherish his,
because in me it bides.

—Sir Philip Sidney

"Good Evening, Naomi." Edward appeared in the study of McDonnally Manor.

"Edward, you're back! When did you arrive?" Naomi's dancing green eyes brightened her already glowing face. Naomi left the easy chair by the window where she was enjoying *The Hound of the Baskervilles*.

"Oh, I have been back for awhile. How have you been, Love?" he shyly placed a kiss on her forehead.

"Fine, thank you. And you?" Naomi returned, still experiencing the newness of their relationship.

"I'm well. I see you have you been keeping yourself occupied since I left?"

"Yes, it's an intriguing book, have you read it?"

"No. Anything else of interest on the home front?"

Naomi paused, letting one strand of deceit escape from her spinnerets. "Nothing of consequence, the usual daily routine."

"The usual routine...Awfully boring, I should think, with the man of your dreams out gallivanting."

"Yes...yes, but of course, there was always Allison and Guillaume to provide me with entertainment... and the puppies on quiet afternoons." Another silken strand escaped as the inescapable web developed.

Edward reached in his coat pocket. "I have something for you, Naomi."

"What is it Edward? Tell me, is it a surprise!"

"Yes, it's a surprise."

"Should I close my eyes?" Naomi's excitement intensified as she squeezed her lids shut and held her hand out to receive the unexpected gift.

Edward removed the present from his pocket and placed it in her hand. Naomi's smile broadened, her chin lowered and her eyes gradually opened to view a small maple box. She stared at it in surprise when Edward coaxed her, "Open it, Love." She lifted the lid to find a handsome pair of jeweled pins, one a cursive letter 'N' and the other, 'M'.

Oh...an "N" and a "M" like on the stone. "They are wonderful, Edward."

"I'd wager that you don't know what they are."

"Why they are monogram pins, of course."

"Not just any pins, Naomi. They are glove pins."

"Glove pins? I don't believe that I have ever seen any."

"Neither had I. I found a jeweler who designs them exclusively to be worn at the wrist of each glove," Edward explained.

"How clever, Edward."

"Let's see how they look, Naomi. Where are your gloves, the black ones?" Naomi went to the hall and checked her coat pockets, only to find one of the pair.

"That's curious, I seemed to have misplaced the mate."

"Where could you have lost it, Naomi?"

"Uh...here, somewhere. I have been here most of the day." Naomi's conscience squirmed with the half truth. *I can't tell him where I was today, he will never understand.*

While revisiting the events of the day, Eloise entered the hall carrying the missing article and offered it to Naomi.

"Thank you Eloise, I was looking for this, I must have dropped it outside." Naomi sighed with relief.

"Don't thank me, Mum. Your stepmother's note implied that one of the dogs at Grimwald found it in the woods," Eloise reported. Naomi stood frozen entrapped by her own words. She felt that any reaction would surely condemn her.

"That is your glove, is it not, Naomi?" Edward asked suspiciously.

"Yes..." Naomi answered, barely above a whisper. She stared at the glove avoiding contact with Eloise or Edward as her invisible web grew. Eloise sensed the tension between the couple and turned to leave when Naomi latched onto her arm.

"Look, Eloise, they're glove pins. Aren't they lovely? Help me put them on," Naomi insisted.

Edward cut in, "Eloise, I'll help her."

"Yes, sir," Eloise exited immediately without question. Naomi swallowed hard, anticipating "fireworks" but not those Eloise described in their recent conversation. Edward placed his hands on Naomi's shoulders and then gently turned her to face him.

"Naomi, why didn't you tell me that you were at Grimwald?" Edward asked innocently. The soft, yet forgiving tone of his disapproval, gave her new strength as broke free from the damning threads.

"I guess I for...oh, *Edward...*" she leaned into his embrace, "I wanted to tell you, but it was confidential. Hiram and I—"

"Hiram!" his grasp tightened slightly on her shoulder, cringing at the thought of her involvement with his nephew and sharing secrets without his knowledge.

She drew back from his grip, pushing him away with tight-fisted hands to his chest and stamped her foot. "You see! That's why I didn't tell you! Edward McDonnally, you make me feel like a common criminal at the mere mention of Hiram's name! And what right do you think you have checking up on me every thirty seconds like some Sherlock Holmes!"

"Every thirty seconds? I'll have you know that I have my own affairs to take care of, without trying to keep track of your dealings!"

"Affairs? Yes, where do you mysteriously slip off to every few weeks? Do you see me interrogating *you* about your clandestine meetings?" she shouted.

"Clandestine meetings! My business meetings are only 'clandestine' because of *your* father. If it weren't for him I would shave off this blasted beard and live like a man, not a scared rabbit. Is it my fault that he is a raving lunatic?"

"Well, you don't have to worry about *my* father, anymore! He's gone!"

"Good! Where?"

"If you would have given me a chance to finish my sentence, I would have explained that Hiram and I are engaged—"

"Aghh!" Edward whirled around with his hands clutching his head and then threw himself down to the divan. Naomi ran to his side, dropping her gloves on the table next to the sofa, and reached to feel his forehead.

"Edward, what's wrong? Are you ill?" She reached for his forehead.

Edward pulled back from her touch. "Am I ill, you dare ask! Engaged! How in the devil can you be engaged when you are still married to *me?*"

"No Edward, no. Again, you didn't let me finish. Hiram and I are engaged in a search for his sister, Hannah." Naomi explained calmly.

Edward lay crumpled for the next minute believing that no greater fool lived. Then he peeked up at the Naomi, standing over him with arms crossed and a look which categorically screamed, 'now, aren't you ashamed of yourself'.

He unbuttoned his tightly clamped lips and nonchalantly commented, "You don't say."

"Yes, I do. Are you ever going to trust me, Edward, McDonnally?"

"Are you going to continue keeping secrets, Naomi?" Naomi shrugged playfully.

"Come here, you sweet thing," he tugged at her skirt then pulled her over down beside him. He leaned over her to kiss her, looked for approval, received a smile and moved his lips to hers and ended their second quarrel.

The passion subsided when Edward straightened to a sitting position, rearranging Naomi beside him and inquired, "A search for Hannah? After all these years?"

"Yes. Hiram wants to find her and I wanted to help. No more secrets. Hiram never told me about Hannah. I discovered a letter, purely by accident, which your brother Geoffrey had written to Amanda about the search for their baby."

"Just where did you *discover* this letter?" he cautiously demanded.

Naomi reluctantly divulged the truth, "In the chest...under the bed...in her room...on the third floor."

"And why were you crawling around under Amanda's bed?" he teased.

I had this same conversation with Hiram. Patience, I was so upset.

"Naomi?"

"It's a long story. "All right, I admit that I had no justification for being in your sister-in-laws room, much less reading her personal correspondence. The fact is, I did."

"Well, your love of mysteries seems to incubate your troubles, Naomi. Any leads?"

"That's where Nathan comes into the picture. I was shopping for Burn's Night when I overheard Nathan and Dagmar arguing over Nathan's contact with Vila."

"Vila Ramsey, the nanny?" Edward asked with surprise.

"Yes, it seems that he has been supporting her for years while she hid in Stockholm."

"That blasted...!" He got up and walked across the room. "What about Hannah?" Edward's face reddened with fury.

"We don't know, Edward. Nathan left Lochmoor with the evidence of his connection and Hiram met with his contacts in Sweden to search for Hannah."

"You should have told me, Naomi. I may have been able to help."

"You were leaving on business and we didn't want to concern you with a search which at the time, had no evidence to build on. Hiram sent a wire from Paris. Hannah, if living, may be there."

Edward walked back and sat beside her. "Naomi, the last time I saw Hannah, I was only nine years old. She was a little bundle of mischief, even more so than Hiram. I remember that last day. She was wearing a little pink gown. Amanda sat her down right there," he pointed to the large over-stuffed chair. "Amanda was trying to tie a pink ribbon around a lock of her hair... Her hair was pitch black and shined like polished obsidian... curly like Hiram's. That little rascal refused to sit still long enough for Amanda to tie it. Hiram sat on my lap, right here and we laughed and laughed watching Hannah shaking her head while Amanda struggled. Amanda became so annoyed with us. She said that we were encouraging Hannah's misbehavior and sent us outside to play... Naomi, she'd be thirty-six years old now. My niece."

"Yes, Edward," she watched as he processed the passage of time.

"Edward?"

"Yes, Naomi?"

"Dagmar told me something else...Edward, I had a sister. I saw her headstone in the woods at Grimwald."

"A sister? Naomi, no one has ever said anything about another child." Edward responded in disbelief, sliding his hand across his bearded chin, absorbing the implications.

"I know. My question is, why not? An older sister, Edward, not my mother's child. Why was my sister's very short life of only a year, kept a secret? My first thought was that the grave was that of baby Hannah's, but once I saw the dates, I knew otherwise. Dagmar knew nothing of my sister until she discovered Nathan taking flowers to the site one morning. He never spoke of her."

"Nathan had another child and know one knew. I guess that really doesn't surprise me, he has always been a very private man with exception to his vendettas. But putting flowers on her grave? How do you feel about that, having a sister? It had to be quite a shock to you."

"It was...I don't know. I suppose I feel cheated, somewhat. A little sad. I always wanted a sister."

Edward placed his arm around Naomi's shoulder offering his sympathy. Naomi opened the jewelry box, still clutched in her hand. She admired the lovely pins.

"Her initials were 'NM' too...Natalia Mackenzie. The pins are beautiful, Edward." She lifted her gloves from the table, removed the pins from the box and attached them to the gloves. Edward watched as she pulled on the gloves, straightening the fingers and then held them out for his approval.

"Very chic."

"Yes they are, Edward. Thank you," she looked up with adoration. Edward took the cue, but as he leaned over to oblige, Naomi jumped up.

"Wait! Stay here, I'll be back in a moment!" Naomi darted from the study and raced upstairs. Edward shook his head and sat back, still not quite accustomed to Naomi's impulsive nature. He was examining the construction of the empty jewel box when Naomi returned, carrying a velvet pouch in her beautifully gloved hands.

Edward stood as she entered the room, surprised to see the unusual item, "What do we have
here?"

"A gift for you, Edward, because you too, are
my magic square." She placed the present in his
large hands. He sat down, when a slight blush lit
his face.

"What is it Naomi?" Naomi took her place beside him on the sofa.

"I have had it for years. Open it," she eagerly
suggested.

"Naomi, I don't know what to say."

"Hurry and open it!"

He pulled open the tassels and removed the
finely tooled leather album from the bag with a look
of unmistaken gratitude and delight. He began leaf-
ing through the pages adorned with treasured
stamps.

"Naomi, you collect stamps, too?" he asked
astounded by the collection.

"No, not really, this was my mother's. Her
employer Mrs. Landseer gave it to her as a ten year
anniversary present. Mummy loved the stamps that
were on the correspondence that she delivered each
day to Mrs. Landseer."

Edward felt a lump forming in his throat and
his eyes began to burn with the touching gesture.
"Naomi, I am deeply honored."

"She would want you to have it, because I
love you Edward. I should have never kept the
search for Hannah from you. Please accept my
apology for I am truly sorry." His fears took flight
when she reached up and slid her fingers through
his bright red-bead massaging the dimples hidden

beneath as she sobbed, "I'm sorry Edward, I love you. You know I love you."

Edward laid the album and the pouch on the table and took Naomi in his arms and kissed her with the true passion of a very gratified and forgiving husband.

"Would you like to go for a ride, Naomi?"

"Up to Duncan Ridge?"

"I'll get the horses."

Chapter XIV

" Estelle "

Who sat and watched
my infant head
When sleeping
in my cradle bed,
And tears of sweet
affection shed?
My mother.

—Jane Taylor

Hiram walked leisurely down the road. He paused to observe two children seated at a table in front of a brick home. They appeared to be playing "shoppies." The younger of the two, a lad of approximately four years of age, was utilizing his mastery with marketing skills. He was selling a small replica of a stove and a set of miniature pots and pans to a girl, probably a few years older than the little boy. A sister and brother he assumed; they shared similar facial features, dark hair and round eyes; their cherub-like cheeks were rosy from the winter chill. The little girl's dark ringlets, tied up with bows that matched her dress hem, bobbed merrily, as she examined the young man's wares. The vendor, donning the typical Eton collar, stood firm in his price with a stern expression.

Watching the children, Hiram slipped back to his youth in London with his Grandmother and uncle, Edward. Edward born to his mother very late in life and Hiram sent from his Scotland home and convalescing mother, were truly closer than most brothers, despite their age difference. Geoffrey, Hiram's father, had explained the circumstances of Hannah's disappearance to his young son after Hiram had complained of his inexplicable sense of loss. Following that discussion, Hiram had often fantasized of afternoons frolicking with his twin.

Hiram's heart lightened with the possibility that, very soon, he too may be enjoying the company of his only sibling. His smile broadened watching the two children chuckling in their adult roles. Once the small actors, became aware of the one man audience, they exchanged concerned looks and then turned simultaneously to glower at the intruder. At that moment, a woman in her late twenties appeared at the door. Taken aback by Hiram's appealing countenance, she paused in amazement. When Hiram gave a friendly tip of his hat, she gathered her children and hastened them inside, reprimanding the boy for leaving the house without his overcoat. After Hiram offered a complimentary nod and a smile to the young mother peeking through the front window, he continued to the shipping office.

On his walk, a cart parked in front of the blacksmith shop caught his eye for it too was inhabited with the likes of two young ones seated in the back. As he approached the younger of the two girls dressed in the typical cotton dresses with the large hems, designed to be lengthened as the children grew, waved energetically.

"Hello, sir!"

The older girl threw her sister a disapproving look for her zealous greeting to the stranger.

"Good afternoon, lassies," Hiram touched the brim of his hat and bowed from the waist. The two girls nodded shyly; the youngest smiling, wide-eyed.

"Are you a prince, sir?" the little blonde asked.

"No, indeed I am not. Are you two young ladies princesses from afar and this your royal coach?" Hiram inquired. The older girl began to giggle as the younger looked with surprise for the mistaken identity.

A small boy of nearly ten caught Hiram's eye through the blacksmith's window when he appeared from the depths of the shop where a number of metal tires, farm implements and cart hubs hung from the rafters. Each item bore a paper label identifying the owner soon to retrieve the repaired item.

The lad slid a small wooden boat with a wallpaper sail across the end of the large table beneath the front window displaying several cookpots and utensils, expertly crafted by the blacksmith. The father of the tiny princesses stood in a heated conference in the adjacent building discussing a matter with both the wheelwright and cartwright. His obvious disgruntlement was of little consequence to his offspring, who were no way affected by the voluminous discussion.

Hiram bid the children farewell and continued to the office to purchase a ticket to France. Contacts had informed him that Vila's daughter had left Sweden years ago and was employed in Paris. His journey was anything but relaxing, contemplating the upcoming meeting with Hannah.

When he arrived in France, he hired a driver to transport him directly to Paris. Once there, the hot meal served at the inn was left untouched and his night nearly sleepless.

The next morning he asked directions to the pub where Vila's daughter, hopefully Hannah, was employed.

Chattering women, stopped in awe to indulge in the visual pleasure of the tourist whose stride was never broken by their attention. Several minutes later he found himself standing in the doorway of the Café Bleu. The melancholy ring to the establishment's name relit his fears to a negative outcome. He hesitated at the pane of the door, noting the only four customers seated at a table on the north side of the room. An older white-bearded man was speaking to two middle-aged men and a younger man, Guillaume's age, over the remnants of their breakfast.

One deep breath and a momentary prayer encouraged Hiram to enter the large room that reeked of an unknown musty odor. Hints of faded 'blue' dotted the room from the wooden booths to the upright piano with the broken left leg. His eyes were drawn immediately to a large life-size portrait of a beautiful young woman; a woman with long black curly tresses and very dark eyes very much like his own. The painting drew him closer, as it was, without a doubt, the spitting image of his mother, Amanda. Hiram studied the features of the rendition that were virtually identical to that of the portrait in his mother's room on the third floor of McDonnally Manor. He had found her and it happened so quickly that the shock seemed to govern every cell of his being. He stood motionless, examining every detail, when a woman entered from the backroom. Hiram turned, awakened by her nearing footsteps.

"Bonjour."

He began his inquiry, "Parlez-vous anglais?" She answered slowly, "Yes."

Hiram re-examined the portrait then looked into the woman's dark eyes, dull with time and stress, set deep within the careworn face encircled by limp strands of black and gray, not so different from that of his late mother's. Her lifeless hair draped over her hefty bare shoulders above the black-lace capped sleeves which cut into her upper arms. The woman looked to the portrait and commented.

"I was much younger then," she lowered her eyes then wiped her damp hand, wet with dishwater from the morning rush, on her blue floral apron and extended her hand to greet him.

"My name is Estelle."

"Of course it is," he concurred solemnly, knowing without a doubt that his journey was over. He gently brought her shriveled hand to his lips and kissed it sweetly.

"My, my, aren't you the gentleman?"

"Could we speak somewhere privately?"

"I really am awfully busy and not interested in any purchases. The noon crowd will arrive soon."

"Madame," Hiram spoke discreetly, "You misunderstand. I merely would like to engage in conversation with you ... private in nature," Hiram offered diplomatically, trying to mask any sense of urgency.

The woman shook her head with annoyance, "I really don't have the time."

Hiram's voice became serious, "I am not leaving until I speak with you." Seeing her startled look with his change in tone he reiterated gently, "If you please, Madame, I only request a brief discussion."

Estelle hesitated then, led Hiram to a small room off the kitchen where a rickety wooden table and two chairs stood amidst bags of stained tablecloths and empty tins.

"We can talk in here," Estelle pointed to a small wooden chair on the opposite side of the table.

"Madame, my name is Hiram McDonnally," he announced as he sat down on the chair across from her. "Are you familiar with the name?"

Estelle stared at Hiram indignantly. "Everyone is familiar with the McDonnally clan. Do you think that I live in a cave?"

"I meant nothing offensive, Madame. Might I inquire as to the health of your mother?" Hiram leaned back in the chair, curiously observing.

"My mother? I haven't seen my mother in years. Don't know if she is living or dead." Estelle answered without a second thought. "Do you know her?"

"Possibly... what would her name be?"

"I don't believe that is your business. Sir, I think you should leave," she commanded. Hiram sat back and closed his eyes.

"Sir?"

Hiram slowly opened his dark eyes now resembling deep pools. He cleared his throat to speak, straightening in the chair. He then made direct eye contact with Estelle. She attempted to look away, disturbed by the intensity of his glare. Hiram remained silent then unbuttoned his black wool overcoat and reached inside the interior pocket and withdrew a folded white handkerchief.

He placed the cloth on the table. Both Hiram and Estelle stared at it. It was the moment of truth for Hiram; there in front of him lay the evidence hidden within the mysterious cloth. Estelle watched curiously, contemplating its contents, when Hiram glanced up, then with trembling fingers directed his attention to unveiling the object hidden within. The unfolded linen presented an antique gold locket. The lid's scrolled design was embellished with two tiny pearls centered within two small diamonds. Hiram lifted the pendant and reached for Estelle's hand. She withdrew it fearfully hesitant.

"Please," he whispered, reaching again for her right hand. His intense plea enticed her to slide her upward palm toward him.

Hiram placed the treasure into her hand as she questioned, "What's this?"

"Please, open it." She gently pressed the release latch and opened the lid. It was as though she was revisiting a chapter of her past. There before her was her own likeness of ten years ago; the same woman in the portrait above the piano in the next room. Across from it was that of a handsome young man in uniform. Estelle sat back in the chair re-examining the locket.

"I have had it for years. It's yours, it belonged to my...our mother, Amanda McDonnally."

"Our mother? You're mistaken. My mother is Vila Ramsey."

"I know that you find this to be an incredible tale, but the fact is, you are Hannah, my sister, my twin sister. You cannot deny the resemblance. I have come to take you home. You can't live this way. You don't have to; you are a McDonnally. Come home with me. You would love it there at the manor." Hiram's optimism guided him.

Yes, I would. We have been there brother, looking for you, years ago she thought despairingly. *It's too late for me.* She grasped the locket and left the chair and turned to the small clouded window overlooking the alley. "I am not going anywhere. You need to leave, before I call the jean d'armes."

"Hannah, please."

"Stop calling me Hannah!"

Hiram stood up shoving the chair behind him. "You were christened Hannah Ruth McDonnally. At nine months, you pulled that very locket from our mother's neck and broke the ring. Our nanny Vila Ramsey kidnapped you in the night and left our parents devastated."

"Stop it! Stop it!"

"Mother never recovered from the loss, she would want you home with your clan."

"I am not a McDonnally! Do I look like a member of high society?"

"You look like our mother, and she was beautiful," Hiram spoke calmly, determined to maintain his composure.

"Get out! I'm not going anywhere, this is where I belong!" the shaken woman left her chair and turned her back to him. Determined, he moved toward her cautiously and reached for her shoulders, when she blurted out, "Don't touch me!"

His hands dropped to his sides. "Ah yes, you are indeed a McDonnally. We come from a long line of stubborn invincible soldiers. No one knows better than I, that a McDonnally cannot be forced against their will." She remained silent, facing the window where she watched a small boy rescuing a mangy pup from a wooden crate beneath a heap of rubbish.

"I didn't mean to upset you. Please keep the locket, it is part of your inheritance and I will honor your decision. I am leaving my address, if you come to your sen— if you change your mind... I'll be leaving now."

Hiram Geoffrey McDonnally had found his twin after thirty-four long years. Now within a quarter hour, she came into and out of his life like a falling star; a beautiful bright flash of hope that would sink beyond the horizon, never to be seen again, leaving doubts to the reality of its momentary existence.

With broken words, he whispered, "Hannah, you are my twin, you will always be part of me. I love you, my sweet sister."

He had dreamed of this day, the day that he would speak those precious sentiments. It was over now; the dream lasted but a moment. Hiram opened his coat and dropped his card on the table. He walked slowly to the doorway agonizing, refusing to turn back. Crushed with disappointment, his anger intensified with each step that became heavier with regret as he approached the café doors. Before his journey's end, his conscience lost ground, unencumbered by his past promise to control his raging temper. Nothing mattered; all rational boundaries gave way to unleash his embittered soul. In one powerful swing he struck the small table before him with both fists then blasted it through the café doors with all his strength and sorrow.

"NO!" he bellowed storming out to the street. He stood heaving every breath amidst the debris at his feet. He pulled a roll of bills from his coat pocket and cast them back to the café floor, stepped over the rubble and began to aimlessly walk the streets of Paris.

No one will ever hear of her conduct, or of her existence, for that matter, he vowed disdainfully.

In the backroom of the Café Bleu, Estelle lay slumped over the wooden table with the locket clenched in her right hand, Hiram's card in the other.

Chapter XV

"Burns' Night"

If I should meet thee
After long years,
How should I greet thee?—
With silence and tears.

—Lord Byron

January twenty-fifth was bitter cold but the tastefully decorated Brachney Hall was warm with hospitality and excitement. Naomi and Edward had spent the last two weeks preparing. They were nearly ready to begin the perfect Burn's Night. Scotland's most festive eve would honor their champion, Robert Burns, tenant farmer, national poet and songwriter. Edward steadied the stool while Naomi tied up the last bit of bunting.

The guests began arriving at six thirty. Each guest was presented to the others with the sounding of Mr. Dugan's bagpipes and all would rise in their honor. Once all the guests were seated, Edward, the chairman, welcomed everyone. He then recited the traditional Selkink grace, however in Scots:

Some has meat and canna eat,
and some wad eat that want it,
but we hae meat and we can eat,
and sae the Lord be thankit.

The evening entertainment began with Hiram's rendition of *My Luve is Like a Red Red Rose*. The audience applauded vigorously, for it was truly sung quite beautifully with his tenor voice. Next, Edward signaled for the procession to begin. The guests stood as Naomi carried in the Haggis on a silver platter to Mr. Dugan's piping. All clapped with the music as the main course was set before Guillaume. The steaming haggis topped the already excellent menu of cock a leekie soup, taties and neeps and Tipsy Laud for dessert..Guillaume stood with the carving knife poised. The music ended with Guillaume prepared to welcome the haggis.

"Ye Pow'rs wha mak mankind your care,
And dish them out their bill o'fare,
Auld Scotland wants nae shrinking ware
That 'jaup in luggies;
But if ye wish her gratefu' prayer
Gie her a haggis!"

The guests applauded with jubilant vitality and began to enjoy the delicious meal. Eloise instinctively left her seat to attend to the quiet tapping at the main door. Naomi intercepted her flight and sent her back to her place with the other guests.

"Eloise, today is your day of leisure, I'll greet the guests," Naomi insisted.

"Thank you," Eloise smiled appreciatively. "I tend to forget that I am not at service."

After another weak rap, the hostess opened the door.

"Good evening, Naomi."

"Dagmar! Welcome, I am so pleased that you could join us." Naomi hugged her stepmother and guided her into the hall. Dagmar handed Naomi a box of freshly made biscuits.

"How sweet of you, Dagmar, thank you. Edward will be pleased too. Let me help you with your coat. The meal is being served now. I have saved a setting for you next to mine."

"Any vord of the tvin?

"No, Hiram went to Paris, but failed to find her."

"I am sorry to hear dat. No sign of Nat'an... Tank you for de invitation, Naomi. Grimvald is quiet dese days."

"Well, you will probably welcome the peacefulness after Burn's Night at Brachney Hall," Naomi assured her while the laughter and chatter from the guests resounded from the dining room.

"I understand that your little visitor at Grimwald found my glove."

"Yah, she's yust a little girl, alone like me."

"What kind of dog is she?"

"I'm not sure, a hunting dog, maybe."

"You should bring her over to play with Heidi some afternoon," Naomi suggested as they entered to join the party.

It wasn't long before Mr. Kilvert, honorary speaker, gave the traditional speech on the life of Robert Burns. Everyone listened attentively then joined Mr. Kilvert in the ending toast paying respect, *To the Immortal Memory of Robert Burns.*

Mr. Dugan took his turn at reciting Burn's *Bonie Doon.* When Joseph got to the final lines, Harriet listened intently and gave her husband a questioning eye.

> Wi' lightsome heart I pu'd a rose
> Frae aff its thorny tree;
> And my fause luver staw my rose
> But left the thorn wi' me."

Mr. Dugan's recitation was followed by the usual toast to the lassies and their contribution to the world. Naomi offered the reply which was creatively brilliant. All the women present cheered, while the men felt that they had met their match.

Burn's Night brought out the usual marked patriotism and solidarity among the participants and dually provided temporary relief from individual problems; the focus being solely directed to the honor of Mr. Burns. However, this year's felicity was tempered by a number of intrusive personal issues.

The evening came to a close with Edward rising to thank the guests for sharing the evening at Brachney Hall. He continued with a special tribute to those family members and friends not in attendance. Harriet and Joseph clasped hands and chose not to look at one another, once again facing the reality that young Tavy had returned to sea duty. He had left the week following St. Andrew's Day and the Dugans sorely missed his presence.

Naomi watched with concern as Hiram's celebratory contentment similarly drifted away, with Edward's sentiments. *I so hoped you would have located Hannah and brought her home,* she thought compassionately.

Hiram shifted in his chair and folded his hands in his lap as he listened, glumly remembering the visit with Estelle, *The perfect evening. Good food, good music, friends and family....perhaps not quite perfect. If you were only here, Hannah.*

Dagmar too, felt a tinge of remorse for her solitary life at Grimwald, although Nathan's intolerable past dealings failed to create any feelings of loss for his absence.

After Allison cleared her throat several times to remove an unknown irritant, she excused herself from the dining area. She left abruptly to the kitchen, embarrassed with her disturbance to the orator. Meanwhile Edward led the arm-locked group in the choral singing of Burn's heartrending *Auld Lang Syne.*

During the final stanza, to the Dugan's delight, Henry McTavish appeared at the parlor doorway with a young woman at his side. The guests sang the last line with renewed energy at the sight of the young Tavy. Harriet began to weep as she ran to hug her surrogate son. The singing stopped as did all conversation with the new arrivals.

The dark eyes of Tavy's lovely companion skipped from face to face till they met the sapphire blues of the handsome Guillaume. Before a word welcomed her, a broad smile of sheer delight lit her face. She stepped forward and spoke softly, "Oft in the stilly night ere slumber's chain has bound me, fond memory brings the light of other days around me."

Naomi glanced toward Edward and then turned quickly in alarm toward her daughter standing in the hall behind the newest guest. Allison's fists were clenched at her side and her eyes narrowed with each word that the girl directed toward her beau.

Guillaume absorbed the recitation in disbelief, swallowed hard, then replied, "The smiles, the tears, of boyhood years, the words of love then spoken; the eyes that shone, now dimmed and gone, the cheerful hearts now broken."

"Guillaume!"

"Sophie!" The exchange of lines ended with the two in a warm embrace with a genuine closeness felt by all the onlookers, including Allison who stood in apparent shock.

Harriet Dugan whispered to Tavy, "Who might this be?"

"I haven't the slightest idea. She was standin' by the door when I arrived. She is verra beautiful," Tavy admitted softly.

All listened intently to the happy couple.

"I can't believe it is really you, Sophie, I thought that I should never see you again."

"Nor, I you, Guillaume."

"You remembered!"

"How could I forget?" She searched the other faces, her dark eyes darting from one to another as she continued with enthusiasm, "Guillaume and Trina were my only English speaking friends in Paris," she recounted. "Oh yes, Trina said to tell you that she would be seeing you soon." Edward looked immediately to Guillaume with the mention of Trina. Likewise, Naomi, Eloise and Albert, simultaneously turned to observe Allison's reaction which was one of astonishment and contempt.

However, Hiram heard nothing of what the new guest was saying; his attention diverted by the girl's shining curls and the twinkling of her eyes. He stood immobile next to Naomi, seemingly mesmerized by an apparition in a fog of confusion. Incongruent thoughts and intangible feelings of familiarity muffled her voice till it was barely audible to his ears. Elizabeth observed an intense side of Hiram that she had not witnessed before.

"Guillaume and I would spend aft—," Sophie's explanation ended abruptly when her eyes met those of the handsome Master of McDonnally Manor. Her gaze was captured in his, until it fell fearfully down to his rich, dark beard on down to his kilt and the shine of his black boots. *You're even more handsome than I imagined,* raced through her mind.

Allison's fuse was lit and ready to explode when the young rival then returned to Hiram's questioning eyes and began to move slowly toward him. Allison watched curiously with the others, relieved that the pretty girl was abandoning her beau. *Hiram? No doubt... every girl is attracted to him,* Allison thought cynically.

Sophie, drawn by certain yet nervous confidence, approached the looming figure standing tall and motionless, as though he were in a trance. Once before him, the young woman looked to him for acceptance. Daring not to reveal her barely controlled emotions, she carefully reached into her coat pocket and then extended her closed gloved hand. She then turned her hand, palm up, slowly uncurling her fingers to reveal the item within. Sophie's lips tightened and her hand began to tremble. Her eyes left Hiram's, momentarily, to direct him with a glimpse at the mysterious treasure which she presented.

Hiram's heart pounded deep within his chest; his breathing increasingly shallow. The appearance of the golden locket introduced a full gambit of emotion. First it was the hair, the familiar eyes, the refined air, and the very common apparel; now, his mother's locket in the trembling hand of a perfect stranger. Hiram's thoughts fell back to the moment he had shown it to Hannah in the very same manner.

Sophie watched and waited, as did the other guests. Finally she spoke, "Hello... hello uncle... Mama said I would find you here. She sends her love and regards. I am Sophia. I am a McDonnally." The room was silent.

Hiram's shadowed countenance was replaced with an expression of infinite joy and gratitude. His large hand closed her gloved fingers over the treasured locket. He brought her hand to his lips and kissed it, then looked down at his beautiful niece with pride and overwhelming approval. Believing this night was truly the perfect night, he held her hands in his and dropped his head in reverence. After a moment of silence he threw back his head and spoke out for all in Heaven and Earth to hear.

"Thank you, dear God, thank you, Hannah!" Hiram nearly smothered the newest McDonnally in a lengthy embrace while the guests cheered and applauded with delight in welcoming the young lady.

After a series of brief introductions to the other family members and friends, Sophie felt quite comfortable with her new family. Naomi and Edward, of course were elated with Sophie's arrival and congregated with the others in the welcoming committee. However, they were equally preoccupied with the unknown story behind the mysterious locket and the whereabouts of Sophie's mother, Hiram's twin sister, Hannah.

Unfortunately, Guillaume was busy with a host of questions from Miss O'Connor, while Tavy basked in the love of his adoptive family. Naomi, seeing her daughter's distress sought to intervene when Edward's hand clutched hers and pulled her aside.

"Not tonight, Naomi," he commanded discreetly, then led her to the library and closed the door behind them. Edward had no intention of letting anyone upset his plans for the remainder of the evening.

"*Edward*," Naomi retaliated.

Edward ignored her comment and asked seriously, "Naomi, do you see that stool?" he pointed to the piece sitting in front of the divan.

"Yes...why, isn't that exactly like the stool at McDonnally Manor?"

"No, it is the stool. I borrowed it."

Naomi failed to see the significance in dragging her away from her daughter in her time of need in order to gain her approval for borrowing the McDonnally stool.

"Edward, it is fine. I am sure that no one will mind. Don't worry."

Again, Edward ignored her input. "Naomi, when I last stood on that stool in the chimney, I said to myself, 'Naomi is such a strong, wonderful woman. Here she is, nearly half my size, protecting me.' I thought, 'How many men are fortunate to find a woman as devoted as this?' Perhaps, *devoted* is not the proper word choice."

You brought me here... to thank me?

"Naomi, please sit on the stool. Wait!" He rushed over to the tall wooden stool and made a few quick brushes across the top to insure its cleanliness.

Naomi had known Edward's behavior to be peculiar at times, but usually with good reason. With this rationale, she lifted her skirt slightly and scooted up onto the stool trying to maintain her balance propping her feet on the bottom rung. As she repositioned herself, Edward became frustrated and apologized.

"Sorry, it's a bit tall. I so wanted this to be perfect." He dropped to one knee beneath her *throne*, with his intentions becoming clearly apparent. He fumbled nervously searching his pockets.

"Oh, Edward," Naomi spoke tenderly.

Edward looked up with a confident grin and brought a white velvet box from his pocket. His large fingers awkwardly lifted the lid and he asked,

"Will you remarry me, my magic square?"

Naomi burst into tears, sobbing uncontrollably to the point that she began to teeter on the stool. Her suitor did not know quite what to think of her unanticipated reaction. A second later Naomi lost her position falling backward. Edward lunged to her rescue. Naomi's shrieked and both fell to the divan as the stool slid out from under her. Naomi's sobs were lost quickly to laughter from the unexpected acrobatics.

"You all right, love?" he asked as they resituated themselves on the divan.

"I'm fine," she smiled ear to ear.

"Well, what's the verdict?" He slid his arm around her and held the open box for her examination. She lifted the delicate ring from the box, turning the band around, admiring the alternating assortment of rubies, sapphires, diamonds, and yes emeralds, the color of her eyes.

"It is exquisite. So feminine," she sniffled.

"Look inside," he encouraged.

She held the ring up and read through a blur of tears, *MMS*, engraved inside the gold band.

She looked deep into his eyes, sparkling with hope, and confirmed, "This is the most wonderful day of my life, Edward McDonnally. I can't imagine a more *perfect* proposal. The answer is *yes*."

Perfect, she said perfect!

And when he cometh home,
he calleth together
his friends and neighbours,
saying unto them,
Rejoice with me;
For I have found my sheep
which was lost.

—*Holy Bible* Luke 15:6

Non-fictional facts referenced in My Magic Square

Queen Elizabeth, starring Sarah Bernhardt
Beatrix Potter's *Peter Rabbit*
Popularity of Game of Darts
Oscar Wilde's *The Importance of Being Earnest*
Vanity Fair magazine
Chinese magic square
Louvre, France
Ganser and mud pants with the typical leather straps
Lichen for the dye New light-weight "spinnie"
Fish gutters and fishing details
Finzean saw mill on the Water o' Feugh in the forest of
Birse at Aberdeenshire
Aberdeen, Edinburgh, Campbeltown
Barnum and Bailey Circus
Drystone dykes and pipeclay flagstone entry
Archaeological find of the fifty –thousand year old Pilt-
down Man, near Lewes (later determined to be a hoax)
Dala Horses
Scotland Yard
Arthur Conan Doyles, *The Hound of the Baskervilles*
Eton Collars Cotton dresses with the large hems, de-
signed to be lengthened as the children grew
Blacksmith shop description
St. Andrew's Day
Robert Burns' *Auld Lang Syne*
Burns' Night and celebrated activities

Poetry Excerpts

Acknowledgements

Crowl, Philip A. The Intelligent Traveller's Guide to Historic Scotland. New York: Congdon & Weed, Inc., 1986.

Grun, Bernard. The Timetables of History: A Horizontal Linkage of People and Events. New York: Simon and Schuster, 1982.

Kidd, Dorothy. To See Ourselves. Edinburgh: HarperCollins, 1992

Kightly, Charles. The Customs and Ceremonies of Britain: An Encyclopaedia of Living Traditions. New York: Thames and Hudson Inc., 1986.

Miller, Christian. A Childhood in Scotland. Edinburgh: Canongate Classic, 1989.

Visual Geography Series. Scotland in Pictures. Minneapolis: Learner Publications Company, 1991.

Webster's New Biographical Dictionary. Springfield: Merriam-Webster Inc, 1988.

A NOTE FROM THE AUTHOR:

*I am a firm believer
that education should be an ongoing endeavor.
I stand by the unwritten law
that education should be entertaining
for young and old alike.
Thus, I incorporate
historic places, people and events
in my novels
for your learning pleasure.*

*With loving thoughts,
Arianna Snow*

To order copies of

My Magic Square

and

Patience, My Dear

Visit the Golden Horse Ltd.
website :

www.ariannaghnovels.com

Watch for the sequel to
My Magic Square!